Without Looking Back

www.kidsatrandomhouse.co.uk

Also by Tabitha Suzuma for older readers:

A Note of Madness

From Where I Stand

A Voice in the Distance

Without Looking Back

Tabitha Suzuma

CORGI BOOKS
in association with The Bodley Head

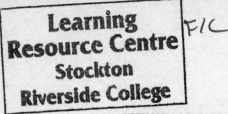
WITHOUT LOOKING BACK
A CORGI BOOK 978 0 552 56000 9

Published in Great Britain by Corgi Books,
an imprint of Random House Children's Books
A Random House Group Company

This edition published 2009

1 3 5 7 9 10 8 6 4 2

Copyright © Tabitha Suzuma, 2009

The Random House Group Limited supports the Forest Stewardship Council (FSC),
the leading international forest certification organization. All our titles that are
printed on Greenpeace-approved FSC-certified paper carry the FSC logo. Our paper
procurement policy can be found at www.rbooks.co.uk/environment.

Set in 10.5/17pt Baskerville by
Falcon Oast Graphic Art Ltd.

Corgi Books are published by Random House Children's Books,
61–63 Uxbridge Road, London W5 5SA

www.kidsatrandomhouse.co.uk
www.rbooks.co.uk

Addresses for companies within The Random House Group Limited can be found at:
www.randomhouse.co.uk/offices.htm

THE RANDOM HOUSE GROUP Limited Reg. No. 954009

A CIP catalogue record for this book is available from the British Library.

Printed in the UK by CPI Bookmarque, Croydon, CR0 4TD.

For Emi, with love

Acknowledgements

A huge thank you to Thalia Suzuma for believing in this book so strongly, Tiggy Suzuma and Tansy Roekaerts for their feedback and encouragement, Akiko Hart for her friendship and support, Dilly Suzuma for the read-through, Linda Davis for being such a great agent, Clare Argar and Sophie Nelson for their invaluable input, Lauren Bennett, Nina Douglas and Ruth Maurice for helping the book reach the readers, Tracey Paris for her talent, patience and hard work, and of course my amazing editor and good friend Charlie Sheppard for always believing in me.

I would also like to thank the real Billy Elliots: Liam Mower, James Lomas, George Maguire, Leon Cooke, Colin Bates and Matthew Koon, who were the inspiration behind *my* dancing boy, Louis.

Prologue

As Louis moved out of the way of the thin stream of people and paused beside the ticket machines to let an old woman by, a poster on the station wall caught his eye. It was a small poster, no bigger than a sheet of A4, and it read: MISSING – HAVE YOU SEEN THESE CHILDREN? in thick black letters. It showed three photographs – a girl and two boys. The girl had long fair hair, a fringe that fell in her eyes and an angelic smile. The first boy had green eyes and shaggy blond hair that came down behind his ears to the nape of his neck, and was squinting at the camera. The second boy wore a blue baseball cap, chunky brown glasses and a lopsided grin. And beneath the photos, in small black print, he read:

Emilie (8 years old), Louis (12) and Maxime Whittaker (14) went missing on 8th June from Paris, France. They are believed to have been abducted by their father, Edward James Whittaker, and taken to the UK. The children's mother has applied for the return of the children to France under the Hague Convention on the Civil Aspects of International Child Abduction. Emilie has a small scar on her chin, likes to suck her middle two fingers, and is known as Millie. Louis has a chipped front tooth and a mole under his left eye; he is sometimes nicknamed Loulou, and is a talented dancer. Maxime is dyslexic, has a small birthmark on the back of his neck, and goes by the name Max.

ANYONE WITH INFORMATION SHOULD CONTACT:
Préfecture de Police, Commissariat Central, Avenue Henri, 75016 Paris, France.
24-hr helpline: +44(0)1 55 43 97 17

A woman pushed past him, muttering angrily to herself. There was a painful thumping sound coming from his chest and he felt as if an invisible hand was closing around his throat. Louis stood rooted to the spot in front of the photo of himself, his brother and his sister, and stared at it in horror.

Chapter One

The scuffed trainer hit the wall with a thud, bounced back onto the bed and lay on its side atop the duvet, inches away from his face. 'Turn it off!'

Louis rolled over and groaned into the pillow. He reached out an arm, swinging his hand optimistically towards the edge of his desk. He made contact with a pile of DVDs, a tall glass and finally his alarm clock. The DVDs and the glass went crashing down onto the carpet; the alarm clock stopped. In his bed on the other side of the room, Max yawned loudly and pulled the covers over his head.

Eyes still closed, Louis raised himself to a sitting position, his feet feeling the carpet for sharp DVD cases. There were none. Only a damp patch from the over-turned glass. He got to his feet, felt his way round to the end of the bed and groped for the door. Morning light was streaming through the curtains and the smell of coffee and the strains of the radio drifted up from downstairs. Louis opened his left eye a crack – enough to guide himself across the landing and into the bathroom. He splashed cold water onto his face and started to yawn, gazing out of the window for a moment, watching a plane trace its way across a pale morning sky. It was the beginning of June. Summer was finally here and the long holidays began in just under a month. With a sigh of satisfaction, Louis returned to the bedroom, picking his jeans up off the floor as he went.

Twenty minutes later, Max was elbowing him out of the way for the last croissant and Millie was spreading an unreasonably large amount of Nutella onto her toast, glancing sideways at Max to check he hadn't noticed.

Max drained his coffee cup and grabbed his school bag from the sideboard. 'Right, I'm out of the door in exactly' – he checked his watch – 'three minutes.'

'Uh-oh, uh-oh!' Millie swung her legs wildly, slurping her hot chocolate.

Max moved towards the kitchen door. 'Two minutes and fifty seconds,' he said, his eyes still on his watch.

'Maman forgot to leave me money for art club again!' Millie exclaimed angrily, going out into the hall to look on the letter table where their mother normally left their snacks and any other bits and bobs for school.

'Two minutes and thirty seconds!'

'Max, Max, she didn't leave me any money—!' Millie looked close to tears.

'All right, all right, calm down,' Louis said. 'I've got five euros – is that enough?'

'Did you have to speak to the judge then?' Pierre asked him breathlessly as they scuffled for the football in the muddy corner of the playground.

Louis got it off him and kicked it hard over to Luc, who scored an easy goal.

'Yeah, but it was OK. I didn't have to stand up in court or anything. The judge just took us into a little room with a video camera. She spoke to each of us in turn.'

'And did you all say the same thing?'

'Of course. We all said we wanted to be able to see Papa whenever we felt like it. Not just one weekend a month. We said that once Papa got his new flat, we wanted to be able to go and stay with him during the school holidays when Maman's working instead of going to summer camp.'

'And what did the judge say?'

'Nothing. She just asked the questions.'

'So, do you get to miss any more school?' Pierre wanted to know.

Louis made a bold attempt at getting the ball off Michel, then fell back. 'No, that's it, unfortunately. The court case is finished.'

When Louis got home after his two-hour dance class, he was starving. Max was boiling pasta again because Maman had forgotten to order any ready meals in her weekly Internet shop at Carrefour. She had another big project at work and was taking clients out to dinner tonight so she wouldn't be back before ten. Millie was doing her homework at the kitchen table amidst pieces of grated cheese, trying to wheedle the answers out of Max. Louis flopped onto the nearest chair and licked his finger and pressed it against the cheese gratings.

'You don't have to just sit there – you could at least lay the table,' Max said grumpily from the cooker.

The idea of getting back to his feet so soon after sitting down did not appeal. 'Can't Millie?'

Max turned and gave Louis an angry look. Then he grabbed the cutlery from the drawer and began laying the table with a lot of clatter, slapping the plates down as if he wanted to break them.

Louis got to his feet. 'It was just a question. I didn't say I wouldn't do it!'

'Bit late now.' Max started dishing up angrily. 'Millie, clear your stuff away.'

Millie scooped up her school books and dumped them on the floor, narrowly missing Trésor's paws. Max sat down, still scowling.

'I got full marks in my spelling test today,' Millie announced proudly, winding some overcooked spaghetti around her fork.

Louis narrowed his eyes at her. 'Liar—'

'I did, I did, I'll show you! The teacher gave me a big gold star.'

'Yeah, yeah, OK, Millie, we believe you,' Max said.

'I want to call Papa. I want to tell him.' Millie pouted.

'You can tell him tomorrow,' Max said.

Millie's eyes brightened. 'Is tomorrow our weekend with him already?'

'Yes,' Louis said.

'Yippee!' Millie crowed.

Seated at the dining-room table, his head propped up on his hand, Louis tried to refocus his eyes on the page of print. Upstairs, Millie was already in bed. From the kitchen next door came the steady hum of the television.

It sounded like *Les Experts*. Louis yawned hard. Max rarely did any homework, which was why he was being threatened with having to stay down a year again. Before Papa had moved out, they had all sat around the table together every evening to do homework, Papa testing Millie on her times tables, Louis on his history dates, Max on his spelling. Max was dyslexic and, ever since Papa had left, seemed to have given up on homework altogether. Only last week he had been talking about leaving school and getting a job once he turned sixteen. That had prompted a row with Maman which had lasted well into the night . . .

The sound of the front door made him start. He tipped forward and narrowly missed banging his head on the table. It was Maman – he could smell her perfume and hear the sound of her heels on the parquet floor.

'*Bonsoir, mon Loulou* . . .' She came in, clutching an umbrella and her briefcase, raindrops speckling the padded shoulders of her dark-blue suit, and kissed him, red wine on her breath. 'What a day! My feet are killing me. Haven't you finished your homework yet?'

He blinked at her blearily. 'History exam tomorrow. Can you test me?'

'Not now, darling. I've got to sit down and I'm dying for a coffee. Where's Max?'

'In the kitchen.'

'Has he done his homework?'

'Dunno.'

'What time did Millie go to bed?'

'Nine-ish.'

'Oh, that's much too late! Maaax . . .?' Her heels clicked down the hallway and into the kitchen.

Louis looked up from his book and stared into space, listening to the rise and fall of the voices from the kitchen. Maman sounded angry, but she was trying to keep her voice down. Max sounded monosyllabic. Discussing homework, or lack of it, no doubt. Maman's job as a broker in one of France's leading trading firms meant she was rarely around to supervise homework. The clock on the mantelpiece read quarter to eleven. Louis closed his eyes again. The thought of crawling into a warm bed was irresistible. Perhaps there would be time to learn that last paragraph at breakfast tomorrow.

Max burst into the bedroom, blinding Louis with the overhead light, kicking off his jeans while grumbling to himself about never being allowed to see the end of *Les Experts*. Louis pulled the duvet over his head to escape from the glare and waited until Max had returned from the bathroom and got into bed before re-emerging. The glow of the streetlamps seeped its way through a gap in the heavy curtains, creating a thin orange shaft on the carpet. Max tossed and turned in his bed, trying to find a comfortable position, yawning loudly. Silence descended.

Louis rolled over onto his side and gazed at his brother's inert figure on the other side of the room. The sound of his breathing had deepened and it would be only minutes before he began to snore.

'Max?'

'Mm?'

'If Papa wins the court case, does that mean we'll be able to start seeing him as much as we want to?' Louis asked.

'No, only every weekend,' Max replied.

'But Papa said he was going to try and get joint custody,' Louis protested. 'I thought that meant three days here with Maman and three days with Papa, with a changeover day in between.'

'That'll never happen,' Max said.

'*Why?*'

'Because . . .' Max heaved a weary sigh. 'Papa told me judges rarely agree to an equal split. They think it's too disruptive to the kids to change house mid-week. The most Papa can hope for is to have us every weekend instead of three days a month.'

'And if Maman wins?'

Another sigh. 'Louis, you know what will happen. Papa talked us through it all again last time we went to stay.'

'But I've forgotten—'

'If Maman wins, then Papa only gets supervised visits, one day a month.'

'But I still don't understand why—'

'Because Maman has told the judge that Papa is mentally unstable.'

'But she doesn't really believe that?'

'No, she doesn't really believe that. But he lost his job because he just stopped going to work after the divorce, remember? He didn't get out of bed for weeks. And she still hates him because he fell in love with that woman . . .'

Louis closed his eyes. 'Yeah . . .'

There was a long silence. 'Anyway' – Max said suddenly – 'even if she does win, I don't care. In a year and a half I'll be sixteen and I'll be able to choose who I live with. Papa said I could go and live with him then and quit school and get a job if I wanted.'

'Don't go,' Louis whispered.

'I'll still be able to come back and see you and stuff.'

Silence.

'Maybe Papa *will* win,' Max said.

There was no time to even open his history book the following morning. Louis had forgotten to set the alarm and was woken by Maman in her bed-hairdo, shouting at them to pack their weekend bags. At breakfast, Max tried it on with the 'I-really-feel-ill-today' routine and Millie cried because she couldn't find her doll. Trying to apply her lipstick using her reflection in the door of the microwave, Maman told Max that if he hadn't bothered to study for his test today he only had himself to blame, then told Millie that she was too old to cry about a doll.

'Is Papa going to pick us up from school?' Millie asked tearfully.

'Yes.' Maman closed her lipstick with a snap and started on her hair. 'Remember to go straight to the gate after class. And if he's late, just wait for him. You know what he's like.'

'Papa said he would take us to EuroDisney again this weekend!' Millie suddenly remembered.

'That's enough Nutella, Millie.'

'He did say that, didn't he, Max?' Millie persisted.

'Probably,' Max replied, spraying croissant c͏ across the table.

'Yippee!'

'Don't come home on Sunday night saying ͏ got homework,' Maman warned.

In the back of the Mercedes, Max wa͏r seat even though it was Louis' turn, and Mille was reunited with her doll amidst whoops of delight. Maman tapped her long, petal-shaped fingernails on the steering wheel in frustration as rivulets ran down the windscreen in front of a sea of red lights. 'My first meeting's at nine. This traffic is a joke!' Suddenly, she glanced at Max and yanked out his earphones. 'I told you not to take that iPod to school.'

'But I want to have my music with me at Papa's!' Max protested.

'Put it away in your rucksack then.'

Max did as he was told, grumbling under his breath.

'Put your books away and take out a blank sheet of paper.'

Louis turned his head slowly to exchange wide-eyed looks with Pierre. There was a shocked silence from the class, followed by general shufflings and mumblings of discontent as textbooks were swapped for blank paper.

Head propped up on his hand in resignation, Pierre was staring sullenly down at the sheet on his desk. He hadn't revised, Louis could tell. As Mr Armand began to write the questions on the board, Louis edged his sheet of paper towards the divide between the two desks and Pierre shot him a grin of thanks.

'Do you want to come over to my house tomorrow to play Tomb Raider?' Pierre asked him later in the playground. They were leaning against the wrought-iron gate and wondering whether they could be bothered to start up one last game of football before the bell rang.

'No – it's our weekend at Papa's,' Louis said.

'Oh.' Pierre pulled some mints out of his pocket, dug one out with his bottom teeth, then held out the stick to Louis. 'Monday after school then?'

'Sure, and I can ring you tomorrow and you can tell me what level you've managed to get up to,' Louis said. 'Papa lets us use the phone for as long as we want at his place.'

'Cool,' Pierre replied.

'Papa, Papa!' Millie dropped her school bag and went hurtling out of the gates. Papa held out his arms and swung her right up above his head. Her hair fanned out behind her; she squealed with delight, then wound her arms about his neck and wrapped her legs around his waist. Papa stumbled forward, Millie still clinging to him like a limpet, and pulled Max towards him. Max grinned and took off his baseball cap and pulled it down over his father's head.

'Look at you!' Papa was saying in English, tilting his head back to see out from under the peak of the cap. 'Max, I can't believe how much you've grown! You're taller than me now! And how's my Louis?'

'I'm good, Papa,' Louis replied, stepping forward to kiss his father. It felt strange to be speaking English again and the words felt uncomfortable in his mouth.

On the train that took them to Papa's flat just outside Paris, Millie chatted nonstop about her good marks at school, her new friend Estelle, and how hard she'd been practising for her piano exam. She swung her legs as she talked, hitting the bottom of the seat with an irritating thump, her eyes dancing with excitement. She spoke in English, but substituted French words whenever necessary, speaking what Papa laughingly referred to as *Franglais*. Papa had always spoken English to them, right from when they were small and he used to stay at home to look after them while Maman went to work – he always said that growing up bilingual was one of the most useful gifts a parent could give a child. But ever since Papa moved out over a year ago, they had been speaking English less and less, and what once was easy had begun to feel like an effort. Whenever Millie broke into French, Papa repeated what she had said in English, as if trying to put the English words back into her mind.

Max started talking about the latest match of his favourite football team, and a film he'd been to see last week at the *Odéon*. Louis suddenly realized that Papa looked tired. He had more lines on his face than Louis remembered, and although he was smiling and nodding at Max with enthusiasm, he looked distant. Then Papa caught Louis' eye and winked.

'How's my dancing boy?'

Louis smiled. 'Good. I've got another competition next weekend in Rouen, on a proper stage and everything. Madame Dubois is going to take me. Luc and Aurélie are coming too. Maman can't make it, so will you come?'

'Of course! Have you managed to nail the triple turn yet?'

'Yes, and my ballet's got pretty good now. Madame Dubois has been really pushing it because she says it's the basis of all forms of dance.'

Max made a snorting noise. Louis glared at him. 'It's not funny! Ballet's really hard – you have to be so strong. It's a sport just like football.'

'Madame Dubois told Maman that Louis is better than all the girls in his class,' Millie pitched in. 'She says he's a natural at ballet.'

'Are you not too intimidated by the girls?' Papa asked Louis with a smile.

'No, they're all right. Anyway, I'm not the only boy in the class – Luc does it too.'

They walked through the quiet streets of Rueil in the late-afternoon sunshine, Papa carrying Millie's rucksack over his shoulder. When they reached his flat on the third floor of an old stone house that stood on the corner of Rue de Rivoir, Millie went charging down the narrow hallway to the kitchen and Papa set her rucksack down by the door. The flat still looked exactly the same as when Papa had first moved in over a year ago. It still had that slightly musty, closed-away smell and, apart from a portable TV, a laptop and a hastily erected clothes rail, contained none of Papa's belongings at all.

In the kitchen, Millie mixed chocolate powder into cold milk, Max switched on the telly and rocked back on one of the kitchen chairs with his trainers up on the table, and Louis helped Papa unpack the three shopping bags on the sideboard. A baguette and a carton of orange juice, a lettuce, some tomatoes, and two frozen pizzas. Louis was surprised. That wasn't nearly enough food to last them all weekend. Max ate like a horse and Millie lived on biscuits. And Louis knew for a fact that Papa's fridge would be completely empty and the dustbin crammed full of ready-meal packets.

'Are you taking us away somewhere for the weekend, Papa?'

Papa looked startled for a moment. Then he cleared his throat, raised his eyebrows and said, 'Yes, yes – how did you guess?'

Millie put down her spoon, splashing chocolate milk onto the table. 'EuroDisney?' she breathed, her eyes wide.

'No, darling, not EuroDisney, not this time.'

Millie's face fell.

'But somewhere else. Somewhere – different.'

'Where?' Millie demanded. Max's gaze shifted from the television screen. Even he suddenly seemed interested.

'Um – well – I'm not going to tell you,' Papa said. 'It's going to be a surprise.'

Millie clapped her hands together. 'I love surprises! When, Papa? Today? Are we going to stay there overnight? Will there be a swimming pool?'

'We're going to leave tomorrow,' Papa said, turning on the oven and unwrapping the pizzas. 'Early. Very early. So I want us to have dinner now and then go to bed. We're going to skip *goûter* and have pizza and salad instead. Then we're going to hit the sack at eight.'

'Are you joking?' Max's eyes widened in outrage. 'I can't go to sleep at eight!'

'What sack?' Millie wanted to know. 'Why do we have to hit a sack?'

'It's an expression,' Louis told her. 'It means go to bed.'

'Go to bed?' Millie squawked. 'Papa, you always let me stay up till Max and Louis go to bed!'

'It's still light at eight o'clock, Papa,' Louis protested.

Their father held up his hands. 'Everyone calm down,' he said, his voice uncharacteristically loud. 'We're all going to bed at eight. Everyone. Even me. It's not up for discussion. We have to get up very, very early tomorrow morning for this surprise visit. And none of you will enjoy it if you haven't had enough sleep.' He dropped his hands and put the pizzas in the oven. He suddenly looked exhausted.

There was silence. Max's eyes swivelled back to the television screen. 'It'd better be worth it,' he muttered.

'It *will* be worth it, Max, I promise.'

'Why do we have to leave so early?' Millie wanted to know.

But Papa just went over to the sink to wash the vegetables and after a while they realized he wasn't going to reply.

After dinner, Max went into the living room to lie on the carpet and play with his PS3 – the PS3 that Papa had bought him last month but Maman wouldn't allow him to keep at home. Millie went into the boxroom to unpack her overnight rucksack and Louis followed her, lying down on her bed and switching on Max's GameBoy. Millie was just hanging up one of her dresses when Papa appeared in the doorway and said quite sharply, 'Don't unpack now, Millie. We'll need all our things with us for the trip and we won't have time to pack again in the morning.'

'Really?' Millie sounded surprised. 'Do we need *everything*?'

But Papa had already gone back to the kitchen. Millie obediently took her dress off the hanger again and put it back in her rucksack. She sat down on the edge of the bed and looked down at Louis. 'Do you think he'll let me unpack my nightie at least?'

Louis glanced reluctantly up from the GameBoy. 'Yes, but don't do it now – take it out at bedtime.'

'I thought bedtime was now.'

Louis glanced out of the window at the evening sun in disbelief. 'Maybe he was just joking . . .' He was doubtful though. Papa looked both tired and on edge. He had held himself back from snapping at Millie earlier, Louis could tell . . . Suddenly, a thought like cold water washed through Louis' brain. It frightened him so much he thought he was going to be sick. He sat up on Millie's bed.

'What?' Millie looked at him, faintly startled. When he didn't reply, she said to him, 'What's the matter, Louis? Your face has gone all pale.'

'Nothing,' Louis said, dropping the GameBoy and getting up off the bed. 'I just need the loo, that's all.'

Apparently satisfied, Millie went back to combing the hair of her new Barbie doll, the one that Papa had bought her last time they'd been to visit. Louis carefully closed the bedroom door behind him and walked quickly down the corridor towards the kitchen. Halfway there, he stopped. The kitchen door was closed, which was unusual. Muted strains of expiring aliens came from the open living-room door. Louis approached the kitchen on tiptoe.

'No, Annette, I haven't told them yet,' Papa was saying in French. 'We only got back home an hour ago. I want to let them settle in first!'

Silence. Louis leaned cautiously against the kitchen door and pressed his ear to it.

'No, that's *not* what this weekend is about! This weekend is about having fun with my kids, damn it!'

Another long silence. Louis could imagine his mother speaking at the other end of the phone, her angry voice like rapid fire.

'We've already discussed this, and I thought we agreed that I would be the one to tell them!' Papa almost shouted.

Another silence.

'Then just give me a chance, will you? They've only been here for an hour! Thanks to you, this is the last weekend I'll have with them. Will you let me break the news to them gently at least?'

Papa said something else, but it was drowned out by the pounding of Louis' heart. He stepped back from the door, fighting for breath.

By the time he heard the receiver slam down, Louis' palms were damp and he could feel a cold sweat breaking out across his back. He took a deep breath and forced his hand up to turn the door handle, wishing his arm hadn't started to shake.

Papa was still sitting at the kitchen table, the phone was back in its cradle and he was massaging his forehead with his fingers, his face red and creased. Louis closed the kitchen door and leaned against it; Papa looked up. 'Loulou, d'you think you could give me a hand with—' And then he broke off. 'What's the matter?' He started to get up.

Louis slowly began to shake his head, and felt his eyes filling with tears.

'Louis . . .' Papa froze, almost comical in his half-standing, half-sitting position. 'Louis – oh, Christ, you were listening?'

He nodded, holding his breath in an attempt to ward off the tears.

'Louis . . .' his father said again, moving out from behind the table and coming towards him. 'Don't – don't— Listen, I don't want the others to know yet.'

Blinking back tears, Louis cupped his hands over his nose and mouth as Papa came forward to grip him tightly by the shoulders. 'Louis, listen – listen to me. Nothing's been decided yet. Maman may still change her mind. I'm going to appeal against the decision. I'm going to fight this – I'm going to fight this, I promise you.' He gave Louis a small shake. His eyes looked desperate, imploring.

'Please, Louis, I really want to wait a bit before I tell the others. I want to enjoy some of this weekend with you without having it hanging over all of us. Don't cry, my darling. It's going to be all right – I promise you it's going to be all right.' His fingers dug into Louis' shoulder blades.

Louis pressed his hands to his face and sniffed hard.

'That's it,' Papa said desperately. 'Come over to the sink and wash your face.'

Louis splashed cold water onto his face while Papa hovered nearby. As he was drying himself with a damp tea towel, he heard the kitchen door open behind him.

'Millie!' Papa exclaimed with false cheer. 'Have you found your Barbie set? Let's go and see what hairstyle you've given her.'

There was a pause, during which Louis rubbed his face hard with the tea towel, carefully keeping his back to the door.

'Wait, Papa,' Millie was saying as Papa presumably tried to usher her out of the kitchen. 'What's the matter with Louis?'

'Nothing!' Papa exclaimed too loudly. 'He just got a—some . . . some soap in his eyes while he was helping me with the washing-up. It's fine, it's all rinsed out now. Where's Max?'

'In the *salon*.'

'Let's go and see if he wants to play a game, shall we?'

'What game?' Millie asked, distracted, and their voices disappeared down the hall.

Louis lowered the tea towel and inhaled slowly, gripping the edge of the sink. He could hear Millie trying to persuade Max into a game of Cluedo. Waves of adrenaline still coursed through his body and it was an effort not to start crying again, but he knew that he mustn't. If he gave the game away now, Millie would sob all night and Max would shut himself in his room and play loud music for the rest of the weekend. But the news took his breath away. He couldn't believe that Maman had won the court case and they were only going to be allowed supervised visits with Papa at some 'family centre' from now on. He couldn't believe that this was the last time they would be coming to Papa's flat, the last time they would be going on a trip together. Maman had said that the supervised visits would only be until Papa had got his life back together again, but the doctor had told Papa he might have to be on anti-depressants for the rest of his life. How would they ever be able to talk to Papa with some stranger sitting in the corner of the room and listening in? It would all be an act, it would all be artificial – they would have to edit everything they said and soon Papa would become a stranger and they probably wouldn't even be able to remember how to speak English any more . . . Suddenly, Louis hated his mother. She kept saying that it was for their own good, that she hadn't trusted Papa since the time he had taken an overdose of sleeping pills and collapsed while they were staying at his flat, but Louis didn't really buy it. She knew how much better he was now. He hadn't fallen apart in front of them for ages. She was still angry with him for falling in love with that woman from work. She just wanted revenge.

'Louis, come and play, pleeease!' It was Millie, calling from the living room. Grabbing a piece of kitchen towel from the roll, Louis blew his nose fiercely, rubbed his eyes a final time and then, taking a calming breath, walked slowly along to the living room.

'I'm Miss Scarlet, Max is Colonel Mustard, Papa's Reverend Green, so who do you want to be?'

They were all seated on the floor around the Cluedo board, waiting for him. Louis knelt down to join them. 'Professor Plum, of course,' he said, forcing a smile.

Half an hour later, when Max discovered that the murder had been committed by Mrs Peacock, with the lead pipe, in the conservatory, Papa said, 'All right, folks. Let's start getting ready for bed.'

'I'm not in the slightest bit tired!' Max exclaimed. 'Oh, come on, let me finish my game!'

'I already said it wasn't negotiable, Max,' Papa said sharply. 'I want everyone to have showered and brushed their teeth in exactly twenty minutes. I'm going to finish the washing-up,' and he left.

On her hands and knees, Millie was carefully putting the pieces away, humming to herself, unbothered by the ridiculously early night and just happy she was getting to go to bed at the same time as everyone else. Max threw himself onto the sofa and switched on his PS3.

'Papa's going to get annoyed,' Louis said.

Max didn't move.

'Max!'

He glanced up, his face angry. 'This is totally un-reasonable of him,' he complained. 'What difference does it make if we go to bed this early? We won't be able to sleep anyway.'

'We can try.'

Millie jumped up. 'Bags I get the bathroom first then,' she said, running out.

Max narrowed his eyes at Louis. 'Why are you taking his side all of a sudden? What's wrong with you anyway?'

'Nothing.' Louis looked quickly down at the carpet and began collecting up the Cluedo pieces that Millie had left behind.

'What's wrong with you?' Max said again.

Louis looked up hotly. 'Nothing!'

'Liar. You've been crying. I can tell. Your eyes were all red when you came in.'

'Oh, shut up,' Louis muttered hurriedly, busying himself with the Cluedo box.

'Fine, don't tell me then.' Max turned back to his PS3.

It was another hour before they finally all got to bed, and even then Max was still grumbling and playing his GameBoy underneath the covers. From the box room next door, they could hear the rise and fall of Papa's voice as he read Millie a bedtime story, and the evening sunlight slanted through the half-closed shutters. Then Papa came in and sat down on the end of Louis' bed.

'Boys, are you packed?'

'Yes.' Max sounded fed up, as if he was tiring of this whole surprise thing already.

'Yes,' Louis said.

'Are you sure? Even your toothbrushes? Have you checked the bathroom?'

'You're beginning to sound like Maman!' Max protested, still playing his GameBoy. 'We're only going away for the weekend.'

'I don't want you to leave anything behind,' Papa said. 'Have you put out your clothes for tomorrow? I'm going to wake you at the last minute, so we'll only have quarter of an hour to leave the house.' He got up, went over to Max's bed and tried to prise the GameBoy from his hands. Max hung on grimly, still fighting with the buttons, saying, 'One more second, one more second, I've nearly killed him!'

'Max . . .' Papa began in a low, warning voice.

'OK, OK!'

Papa bent down to kiss him. Max grumbled and complained that there was no way in hell he was going to be able to fall asleep. Then Papa came over to Louis' bed.

'Night-night, Louis.'

As Papa bent over him, Louis reached up round his father's neck and pulled him close. He breathed in his warm, slightly sweaty smell. He never wanted to let go.

'It'll be all right, Loulou,' Papa whispered in his ear. 'It'll be all right. I promise.'

Chapter Two

'Come on, everyone, up, up!' The overhead light snapped on, blinding them, and Louis groaned and pulled the duvet over his head. But within seconds, Papa was pulling it off him, right off him, and tugging his arm.

'Come on, Louis, go and wash your face right now. Come on, come on!' Papa's voice was low, urgent, forcing Louis to get out of bed and try and open his eyes against the harsh artificial light.

In Max's bed, a battle was waging – Max trying to bury himself under the covers, Papa trying to drag him out.

Louis staggered to the bathroom, started to pee, then opened his eyes fully to look out of the small bathroom window – and saw that it was still night.

Millie burst in before he had even finished. 'Hey!'

'It's today, it's today, we're going on a surprise trip today!' she sang, turning on the tap and splashing her face vigorously.

'It's not even morning – look, it's still dark outside,' Louis said, flushing the toilet and joining Millie at the washbasin. He peered at the radio clock on the top of the medicine cabinet. 'Papa was lying! It's not morning, it's three o'clock at night!'

'It's three o'clock in the morning, so he wasn't lying, it *is* morning,' Millie countered, drying her face on the hand towel. 'Are we going to go out when it's still dark? Ooh, this is like an adventure!'

Suddenly, Max staggered in, his eyes still half closed, his hair on end. 'Get out of here, children, unless you want to watch me do a poo!'

'Oh, yuck!' Millie squealed, racing out.

Before following her, Louis turned to Max. 'It's three o'clock in the morning,' he told him. 'Where could Papa be taking us in the middle of the night?'

But Max just sat on the edge of the bath and started to yawn.

At breakfast, only Millie looked awake, swinging her legs and chattering non stop about where they might be heading. She seemed to be hoping it might still turn out to be EuroDisney. She was dressed in her favourite new outfit – the pink velvet trousers and sleeveless white top – and her hair was brushed away from her face and fastened neatly with a clip on the back of her head. Papa had had a hand in the hairstyle, Louis could tell. Max wore clean jeans, his usual football sweatshirt and matching baseball cap. His head, propped up on his hand, looked in danger of falling onto his plate. Papa stood at the table, uncharacteristically smart in khaki trousers, polished shoes and a dark-green v-neck, his hair wet and neatly combed back, displaying a receding hairline. He had already lined up their rucksacks by the front door and was conducting this breakfast military-style, cutting up the baguette and spreading the butter and pouring the hot chocolate, appearing to be trying to get them all to eat as much as possible in the shortest space of time. It was, in essence, breakfast in the middle of the night, and Louis was finding it difficult to get anything down. Papa himself wasn't eating anything, Louis noticed, but he was already on this third cup of black coffee and his eyes seemed to be on fast-forward.

When none of them could manage another mouthful, Papa cleared the table, put all the leftovers in the bin and told them to go to the loo while he took out the rubbish. When he returned, he went round the flat, turning off switches and checking under their beds and insisting that Millie wore a jumper even though she pointed out that it was summer. Then they picked up their rucksacks and went down the staircase and out into the cold night air.

The street was lamp-lit and deserted and Papa started walking very fast, and when Millie tried to ask a question, he told them that he needed them all to be quiet for a while. Two streets away, he approached a car parked at the kerb with its engine still running and a small light visible from inside. Papa threw open the passenger door and motioned for them to get in.

It wasn't a taxi, at least not a regular one, because it had no sign on the top of it. Millie started to say something, then stopped herself, and climbed in silently. Max hung back, fiddling with his iPod, and told Louis in no uncertain terms that he wasn't going to sit in the middle.

'Why do I always have to sit in the middle?' Louis protested.

'Tell Millie to sit in the middle.'

'Why can't you?'

'Get *in*!' Papa said, in a voice that left no room for argument.

The driver was a man that Louis vaguely recognized – an old friend of Papa's perhaps? But he didn't introduce himself; in fact, he didn't say anything much at all as they all squashed uncomfortably in the back seat, their rucksacks on their laps. He drove very fast and very badly, taking lots of little side roads, so that it wasn't long before Millie started to complain about feeling sick. But to Louis' surprise, Papa didn't ask the man to pull over. He just stared ahead fixedly. And the hand that gripped the door handle was white.

'I'm going to be sick,' Millie declared miserably to no one in particular. 'It's going to go all over everyone and all over this man's car and then everyone's going to be mad at me.'

'Try and think of something else,' Louis suggested. 'How about all the words you can think of that begin with *p*?'

'Can't think of any,' she moaned.

Max had his eyes closed and his head against the window, the music buzzing in his earphones. In the front, Papa and the man talked in hushed, low voices. Louis found himself hoping the trip would improve.

It did improve once they got out of the car, because they found that they had arrived at Charles de Gaulle Airport, and the real excitement began to kick in.

'Are we going to Cork?' Millie squealed, bounding up and down at the end of Papa's arm as they waited in the queue for the check-in. 'Are we going to visit Grandma and Granddad?'

'It's a surprise,' Papa said firmly.

When they reached the check-in counter, Louis saw that Papa was holding their passports. So Maman must have been in on this too! Maman wasn't usually any good at keeping surprises but she had certainly succeeded this time! Perhaps she was beginning to forgive Papa after all?

Louis could feel the butterflies start in his stomach as Papa's eyes scoured the departure screen. Louis followed his gaze and saw that there were only two flights leaving the airport in the next hour – one for Stockholm and one for Amsterdam. Max had noticed too, and he shot Louis a delighted grin. They had never been to Sweden or Holland before.

In the near-empty departure lounge, none of them could sit still. Millie danced from foot to foot at the window, watching a plane take off. Max dribbled an empty can of Coke across the shiny floor. Louis made the most of the slippery surface to practise his triple spin and earned himself some applause from a young couple sitting in a corner. Then Papa told them sharply to come and sit down. However, it wasn't long before flight two-four-six to Amsterdam was called, and Papa jumped to his feet and told them to hurry. Max spun round to grin at Louis and exclaim, 'No way!'

They proceeded quickly onto the plane. It felt strange boarding a plane so early in the morning and Louis felt his insides fizz with excitement as they stepped off the mobile corridor and into the loud humming mouth of the aircraft, even though Papa still hadn't smiled since he'd woken them up.

When they got to their seats, Millie bounced up and down. Louis was having a hard time containing his own excitement and kept glancing at Papa to try and glean some idea of what he had in store for them. But his expression was preoccupied, distant, and when Millie jiggled up and down in her seat singing, 'We're going to Amsterdam, we're going to Amsterdam,' he told her sharply to stop it. Once they were airborne, however, he seemed to relax slightly and ordered a black coffee from the stewardess, then glanced over at Max with a hopeful smile and said, 'So, was this worth going to bed early for?'

'Definitely!' Max answered with a grin. 'Wait till I tell the others on Monday!' He stopped for a moment. 'Hey, Sunday's tomorrow. Are we just staying there one night?'

'We're staying for a week,' Papa said. 'I've booked you a week off school.'

'Oh, wow! Oh, yes!' Millie squealed.

'Cool, Papa!' Max exclaimed. 'A whole week! Oh, you're the best!'

Louis thought for a moment. He was supposed to be going to Pierre's on Monday after school. On Tuesday he had his street-dance class, on Thursday he had ballet, on Saturday mornings he had tap and there was a competition he was supposed to be going to in the afternoon. His teacher would be furious. But he forced a smile and said, 'That's great!'

When they landed in Amsterdam, a light drizzle was falling. They had all eaten second breakfasts on the plane. Louis suddenly felt very sleepy and he wondered whether there would be any chance of having a rest before Papa started them on what would typically be an activity-packed schedule. But to his surprise, his father said that they would be going straight to the hotel.

They caught a taxi from the rank outside the airport and Papa spoke briefly and sparingly to the driver in English. Normally he was keen to engage in conversation with anyone who crossed his path, finding out details of a complete stranger's life only seconds after meeting them, but since coming off the plane he seemed to have gone very quiet. Millie insisted they all play I-Spy, but Papa didn't join in.

When they reached the hotel, they emerged from the taxi into the pale grey Amsterdam morning. The hotel was small, tucked away on a narrow cobbled street, and Papa had booked them all into one room.

As soon as they went in, Max flopped down onto the first of two big double beds and switched on the TV, Millie had a conversation with herself about which bed she was going to sleep in, and Louis went to look out of the window.

'Come away from the window, Louis,' Papa said. 'And, Max, switch off the television for a moment. I want to talk to you.'

'I like this bed best,' Millie declared, plonking herself down cross-legged in the middle of it. 'It's more bouncy.'

'This TV's crap,' Max complained. 'It's all in Dutch – they don't even have CNN.'

'Switch off the television.' Papa sounded like he was trying to hang onto his temper. 'Louis and Millie, come over here.' He sat heavily down on the edge of the bed. Max flicked off the television with a scowl. Louis sat down on the second double bed next to Millie.

'Right,' Papa said. He took a deep breath. 'Now listen up. I've got to go out for a while. To sort out some things for the – er – the surprise.'

'You mean Amsterdam isn't the surprise?' Max asked.

'Not the whole surprise, no,' Papa answered. 'Now listen. I want you to promise to stay in this room till I get back. This is not a very safe area and so it's imperative that you don't go out without me. Is that understood?'

'What does imperative mean?' Millie wanted to know.

'Very, very important,' Papa said.

'Oh.'

'Now, is that a promise?'

'How long will you be gone?' Louis asked.

'Not long. Two hours, maybe three.'

'And when you get back, can we all go out together?' Max wanted to know.

'Well, we'll see,' Papa answered evasively.

'What are we going to do for three hours?' Max protested. 'We haven't even got a decent TV!'

'Read a book or something,' Papa snapped. 'Now I want you to promise.'

'OK . . . Yes . . . We promise,' they all said.

'Are we going to sleep all together in this room all week?' Max asked.

'No. Tomorrow morning we're going somewhere else.'

'Tomorrow?' Millie's eyes lit up.

'Yes, very early tomorrow morning, so we'll have another early night tonight,' Papa said, getting up and taking some things out of his rucksack. 'The room-service menu's over there. If you get hungry or thirsty, order anything you like. You just have to pick up the phone and dial one for reception.'

He left, checking and double checking his pockets as he went. Max turned on the television again and started fiddling with the aerial. Millie sat on the living-room carpet, drawing picture after picture for a mural on her bedroom wall. Bored, Louis pushed one of the beds over to the wall and practised doing handsprings and back-flips while Millie complained about the room shaking.

'You've jogged me *again*, Louis – now the cat's tail's gone all wrong!'

Louis took a break from the tumbling and switched to some fast *fouettés*, his spinning body making Millie's loose drawings billow up from the floor. But this time she didn't object and paused in her drawing to gaze up at him.

'Wow. Do that jump where you spin around in the air!'

He obliged. After he landed, a picture fell off the wall.

'Louis, you're not allowed to practise inside!' Max complained from the bed.

'Your name isn't Dad!' Louis retorted.

'Do that jump where you do the splits in the air,' Millie continued.

He obliged, nearly impaling himself on the corner of the television.

Millie put the cap back on her felt-tip and stood up. 'Teach me?'

It was a game they played at home in Paris. On dance nights, after his class, Louis would come home and attempt to teach Millie some of the new moves he'd learned that day. 'I'll teach you the new routine,' he said, fiddling with the bedside radio to find appropriate music. 'Ready?'

Millie nodded eagerly, poised, her feet pressed together. The radio blasted out a strong dance beat and Louis took up his position in front of Millie. 'Five, six, seven, eight . . .'

But two hours later, serious boredom was beginning to set in. They had ordered club sandwiches and chocolate éclairs and tall glasses of Coke, and eaten until they felt ready to throw up. Millie had rearranged her clothes on the narrow cupboard rail more than a dozen times, and was now using her Barbie doll to try and tickle Max's feet. Max was gazing dully at a Dutch TV programme, every now and again breaking off to yell at her. Louis lay face down on the second bed, his eyes half closed, his finger tracing a pattern on the mottled carpet. Then a thought occurred to him. He could use Max's phone to send a text message to Pierre. His mouth would fall open when he read they were in Amsterdam. Louis didn't need to tell him that they were stuck in a hotel room, with Papa acting strange again. Just that they had been whisked away for a surprise holiday. Pierre would be so jealous . . .

Max gestured languidly to his jacket when Louis asked him if he could borrow his phone. Louis crossed over to the chair and put his hands in the pockets for Max's mobile. It wasn't there. He tried each pocket in turn. Empty, apart from some euros, a train ticket, and a mint with bits of fluff stuck to it. 'Your phone's not there.'

There was a shocked silence. Then Max levered himself slowly up from the bed, his eyes narrowing. 'If this is your idea of a joke . . .'

Louis said nothing – just held out Max's jacket for him. Max went through the pockets again. 'No way! No way!' he exclaimed loudly.

'Try your rucksack,' Louis suggested.

Inhaling sharply, Max grabbed his rucksack and started emptying it onto the floor. Then he grabbed Louis'.

'Hey, I haven't taken it!'

By now the hotel room was looking like a bomb had

hit it. 'Oh, this is great!' Max started to shout. 'Just great! No wonder Papa doesn't want us to go outside. This place is full of crooks!'

'Maybe you left it in the flat.'

'No, I had it on the plane! I used it to check the time!'

'Maybe you were pickpocketed on the plane. Or maybe you left it on the seat . . .'

Millie's eyes were wide. 'Maman's going to be soooo mad,' she murmured.

Still looking around the room wildly, Max's eyes fell on the phone on the bedside table. 'D'you know Papa's mobile number by heart?' he asked Louis.

'I do,' Millie said.

Max grabbed the receiver and pressed one of the buttons. 'Hello, can you give me an outside line please?'

Louis watched him. There was a silence. Max sat down heavily on the edge of the bed, running a hand through his hair. His mobile phone was one of his most prized possessions. He'd only had it since his fourteenth birthday. Suddenly, he sprang to his feet.

'Who is Mr Franklin? It's Mr Whittaker, room one-four-six! I'm his son. I just want to call him!'

Another long silence. Twittering at the end of the line. Max's eyes were growing wider and he was breathing very fast.

'But I need to speak to him! I'm his son! It's an emergency – we've been pickpocketed!'

Another silence. Then Max slammed down the phone, making them all jump.

'What?' Louis said instantly.

Max sat down again and rested his elbows on his knees, looking up at Louis in amazement. 'Papa's barred all outgoing phone calls!'

'What?' Louis said again.

'Yeah, it's unbelievable. The woman said that Mr Franklin had forbidden any outgoing phone calls from this room! When I said there was no Mr Franklin staying in this room, she said that she was sorry, but that was the name the man who'd checked in with the three kids had given!'

'Maybe there was another family and she got the names confused,' Louis suggested.

'We're practically the only people in this whole hotel,' Max retorted. 'I haven't seen any other families around. Have you?'

'No, but—'

'You know what this means, don't you?' Max glared at Louis, but his eyes looked frightened.

'Don't say it—'

'Papa's going mad again.'

There was a silence, broken only by Millie, who during the course of this exchange had been admiring herself in the full-length mirror. Suddenly, she seemed to register what Max had said and slowly turned to face them.

'Papa's not going mad. You're horrible, Max. Papa never went mad!'

'Well he certainly isn't acting very sane!' Max began to shout. 'He whisks us off to Amsterdam in the middle of the night, then holes us up in some dodgy hotel using a fake name, then nicks my new mobile and bans all outgoing calls from the hotel while he goes running about the streets!'

Millie's lower lip began to quiver. 'You're just angry because he went away! You just want to believe all the bad things that Maman says about him!'

'We don't know that he's taken your mobile—' Louis tried to reason.

'Oh, come on!' Max shouted, running his hands through his hair. 'Wake up, people! My mobile has suddenly disappeared and we can't make outgoing calls. Are you trying to tell me that's just some kind of freakish coincidence?'

Millie had begun to whimper now, her two middle fingers in her mouth.

Louis shot Max an angry look. 'Do you think this is helping?'

Max threw himself face down onto one of the beds. 'Fine, fine.' He held out a conciliatory arm towards Millie. 'I was only joking – of course Papa's not mad. He's just a bit weird, that's all. Come here and I'll tell you a story, Millie.'

With a small smile, Millie wiped her eyes and snuggled down on the bed beside him. Louis went back to stand at the window, looking down into the street for Papa. He'd come back to get them, wouldn't he? He wouldn't leave them locked up here for ever?

When Papa did come back, half an hour into Max's story about an intergalactic war, even Max couldn't stay mad at him for long. He was carrying two gigantic pizza boxes, a bottle of lemonade and a stack of DVDs. Max threw himself on the DVDs, Millie started opening the pizza boxes, and Papa told them he had booked them all tickets to another secret destination the following morning. While Louis set up Papa's laptop and Millie started on the pizza, Max told Papa about his missing phone and the strange conversation with the hotel receptionist.

'Oh, I'm sorry about that,' Papa said. 'I took your mobile and locked it up in that little safe – there, under the desk, with the passports and money. You never know in these hotels – things go missing all the time. I think I'll hold onto it for safekeeping until we're back from holiday. I don't want you to lose it, especially as it's such a good one; you won't be able to use it now we're outside France, anyway.'

'So why did the receptionist say we couldn't make calls from the landline?' Max asked with his mouth full. 'And why did she say you'd given a different name?'

'She must have got us muddled up with that family on the floor below,' Papa said easily. 'As I was going out, I heard the dad say that he didn't want his kids to be allowed to run up the phone bill any more.' He caught Louis' gaze and gave him a bright, hopeful smile.

But Max had turned to the laptop and was discussing which film they ought to watch first. Millie was already on her second slice of pizza. Papa started pouring lemonade into their empty Coke glasses and Louis sat back against the headboard, his arms wrapped around his knees. He felt cold suddenly. When he had been looking around the room earlier, bored out of his mind, he had come across the little red safe, nestled into one of the desk drawers. And idly, he had flicked it open. It had been completely empty.

Chapter Three

When they arrived back at Amsterdam airport, it still felt like night despite the weak dawn struggling through the heavy clouds. They had gone to bed after dinner, restless and headachy from a day spent cooped up in just one room doing nothing but eating and watching TV, had found it hard to get to sleep and even harder to get up in the early hours again. However, they were all excited at the prospect of another, hopefully more promising destination. The day before, Louis had been trying to work out which flight could necessitate a stopoff in Amsterdam. It could be anywhere, really.

Inside the almost-empty terminal, Millie did her rubber-ball act at the end of Papa's arm while they waited to check in. Max and Louis went off to scour the departure screens to try and guess which flight was theirs. When they got back, Papa and Millie were hurtling down towards the exit. Louis and Max broke into a run to catch them up.

'Hey, what's going on?'

Papa swung round. 'Where *were* you?' he almost shouted.

'Checking out the departure boards,' Max replied. 'Where d'you think?'

Papa let go of Millie's hand and grabbed Max and Louis by the arm. 'Don't go wandering off without me! I told you we had to stay together at all times! It's not safe, do you hear?'

Louis was surprised by the strength of Papa's grip on the top of his arm. Max pulled away angrily. 'All right, keep your hair on!'

They boarded the plane in silence. Even Millie was quiet. Papa's face was pale and a thin film of sweat had broken out across his forehead. Louis began to wish they were staying in Amsterdam. On the plane, Max let Millie have the window seat without a word and they all sat down. A few other passengers trickled on, but the aircraft was almost empty. Then, as the plane taxied out onto the runway, the pilot's voice came over on the loudspeaker. 'Welcome aboard this Boeing seven-four-seven on flight three-oh-six to London Heathrow.'

Max turned to Papa in amazement. 'We're going to England?'

Papa smiled at long last. 'Yes.'

'Oh, wow!' Millie exclaimed. 'Are we going to see Big Ben? Are we going to see the Houses of Parliament? Are we going to see the Queen?'

Papa allowed himself a brief chuckle. 'Yes, I'm sure we'll get round to doing all that eventually, Millie.'

'Cool!' Max and Millie exclaimed together.

Papa looked at Louis. 'You're very quiet, my Louis. What are you thinking?'

Louis managed a smile. 'I think it's great, Papa.'

During the flight, Papa dozed. He looked very tired and old suddenly. The air hostess brought Millie some colouring things. They ate breakfast off plastic trays and left Papa to sleep. A large middle-aged lady in the seat across the aisle engaged Max in conversation – initially in Dutch, but when Max pulled a face and laughed, she switched to English.

'Where do you come from?' the lady asked Max.

'France,' Max replied.

'Paris?'

'Yes.'

'And what are you doing on a flight from Amsterdam to London?'

'We're on holiday,' Max replied. 'It's some kind of surprise.'

'Is your dad English?'

'No, he's Irish. Usually we go to Ireland to visit our grandparents. We've never been to England before—'

Suddenly, Papa woke up with a start. 'Max!'

'What?'

'I need to talk to you,' Papa said. He looked pointedly at the Dutch lady until she turned away uncomfortably.

'I'd prefer it if you didn't talk to strangers,' Papa said in a low voice.

'But why?' Max protested. 'You're always—' He broke off. Louis guessed he had been going to say 'talking to strangers', but this wasn't true any more. Papa hadn't struck up a conversation with anyone since they had left Paris.

When the plane landed, they zipped through the airport, Millie running ahead, leaving the other passengers behind at the conveyor belt. Heathrow was huge, shiny and absolutely full of people. Papa started to look tense again, insisting that Millie hold his hand. After a brief glance through the sliding glass doors at a white sky, low-flying planes and chaotic taxi rank, Papa led them down the escalator towards the sign that read UNDERGROUND with a red O and a line going through it. He bought them all tickets from the ticket machine as people with suitcases and huge rucksacks jostled all around. Going through the ticket barriers was a bit of a nightmare – Max got his rucksack stuck and had to be rescued by the smiling gentleman behind, then Millie missed her chance and stayed on the other side. Panicked, she ducked under the barrier and crawled out on her hands and knees. They went down to the platform, which was dirty, cold and grey – a bit like the Métro platforms in Paris but shorter. Different languages were being spoken all around – only for a second did Louis catch some English. A crackling, incomprehensible voice rang out over the loudspeaker and Louis caught only one word: 'delays'.

On the tube, there was nowhere to sit and the carriages didn't have those collapsible seats like they did in Paris. Max put his rucksack down against the plastic wall and sat on it, and after a moment Louis did the same. Millie clung to Papa as he swayed about, gripping the overhead rail. Eventually a seat became available and Papa collapsed gratefully into it, pulling Millie onto his lap. Three stops later and the double seat opposite them became vacant and Max and Louis went to join them. By now, the black tunnel they had been hurtling through had been replaced by houses – well, the backs of houses, and some small green gardens with washing lines. They went over a bridge and Millie spotted a red bus and pointed it out excitedly, and there then ensued a rather heated debate about the differences between French and English buses. As was customary when Papa wasn't participating in the conversation, they spoke to each other in French, and Max was just trying to explain to Millie the differences between the French and English transport system, when Louis noticed a woman on the other side of the carriage looking at them with a smile. Papa seemed to notice her too, but instead of turning round and engaging her in conversation, he motioned for Max to quieten down.

When the woman got off at the next stop, the carriage was almost empty, and Papa suddenly said, 'Now that we're in England, how about we pretend to be an English family?'

Millie looked at him, her eyes widening. 'You mean no more French?'

'Why not?' Papa said with a smile and a casual shrug. 'It's the perfect opportunity for you to brush up your English and discover what it's like to be English children for a change. In fact, we could turn it into a game. A five p fine for anyone who says a French word!' He gave a short sharp laugh.

'I only have euros,' Louis informed him coldly.

'I'll give you some English pocket money later,' Papa said.

'What's a p?' Millie wanted to know.

'It's like a *centime*,' Louis told her.

'Bzz. French word! You lose five p!' Papa exclaimed.

'So that means we have to call you Dad?' Max sounded aghast.

'Absolutely!'

'OK then . . . *Dad*.' Max looked as if he hated the word.

The train journey seemed to last for ever. No one seemed to feel much like talking now that Papa, or rather *Dad*, had suggested this bizarre game. Louis felt annoyed that Dad had said he had to lose 5p when all he'd been doing was help explain the concept to Millie, but he knew that his annoyance was a cover-up for a deeper, unsettled feeling that had begun in the pit of his stomach ever since they had left Dad's flat two nights ago. He didn't think that Dad was getting depressed again – his eyes weren't glazed over with that empty look and his face didn't have that hang-dog, exhausted expression. But there was definitely something strange about him. Ever since he had picked them up from school on Friday, he'd seemed wired, jittery, and his behaviour – snapping at them, leaving them cooped up in a hotel room, lying about the mobile phone, and now insisting that they stopped speaking French – was totally uncharacteristic. Louis suddenly felt very tired. He wished he could speak to Max about the phone call he had overheard the night before they left. His thoughts kept returning to it, prodding at it like a sore cut you just can't leave alone. Could this be their last holiday with Dad? Would they really never be allowed to be alone with him again? And why had the judge ruled in Maman's favour? Just because Dad had lost his job and stayed in bed for three weeks after the divorce didn't mean he couldn't be trusted with his own kids!

They got off the blue line at a stop called South Harrow, and when they climbed the long flight of steps and emerged into the weak morning sunlight, there was a car waiting for them outside. A woman jumped out of the driver's side and gave Dad a long fierce hug. Louis and Max exchanged startled glances.

Then the woman stepped back and gazed at Louis, Max and Millie with a slow smile. 'Oh my God, I can't believe it,' she said in a very English accent. 'These are your children, Eddie?'

'Let's get home and then we'll do the introductions,' Dad said, still sounding tense.

The car journey lasted a good half-hour, and on the way, Louis noticed they passed several more tube stations, which made him wonder why they hadn't got off at a closer one. Max was plugged into his earphones again and Millie was sucking her fingers – Louis noticed that there were violet shadows beneath her eyes. They parked in a small street outside a row of terraced houses, and Dad's friend led them to a red door, then through a narrow hallway and into a kitchen. They all sat around a large chipped oak table, catatonic with exhaustion. The woman put on the kettle and set out a large plate of sandwiches shaped like triangles.

Dad said, 'Oh, Meg, it's so kind of you to be doing this – you'll never know how grateful I am . . .'

And Meg said, 'Don't be silly, Eddie. You know I would do anything for you.' She started pouring the tea. 'It's so lovely to see you again, and look at these beautiful children! Let me guess . . .' She looked at Millie. 'You must be Millie.'

Millie smiled and nodded shyly, leaning in towards Max.

Meg looked at Max and said, 'And you must be Max – or is it Louis?' She looked momentarily confused.

'I'm Max, I'm the eldest,' Max said. 'And he's Louis.' He pointed.

'Oh, they've got French accents, you never told me!' Meg exclaimed.

Max cheeks went pink and he scowled down at the table.

'Well I'm hoping they'll acquire English accents as soon as possible,' Dad said.

Several sandwiches and strange chocolate jelly biscuits later, Millie had begun to thaw and was telling Meg in great detail about her kitten, Trésor. Dad was on his third cup of tea and beginning to look more relaxed. Max had taken his GameBoy out of his pocket and was playing it unashamedly at the table. Louis' head felt so full of questions, it ached. He couldn't wait to get Dad alone.

After a while, Meg took them upstairs and showed them where they would be sleeping. Louis and Max would be sharing a bunk bed in one small pink room. Meg apologized for the colour of the walls and said the room used to belong to her daughters, now away at university. Millie's room was in the attic. She had to climb a ladder to reach it and the ceiling sloped so low, you couldn't stand up. But she seemed thrilled with it all the same. Dad and Meg got into an argument over which of them was going to sleep on the sofa bed in the lounge and their voices drifted back downstairs again. Max bagged the top bunk and swung himself up without using the ladder. The bed creaked ominously. Louis sat down on the carpet and rested his arms on his knees, his back against the wall.

Max looked down at him. 'You can have the top bunk if you're going to sulk about it!'

Louis looked up at him. 'I'm not sulking,' he replied. 'I don't care which bed I sleep in.'

Max rolled onto his side and dangled his arm down from the bed, looking unconvinced. 'What's the matter with you then? You've hardly said a word since we arrived.'

Louis rubbed his eyes. His whole body seemed to ache. 'We're supposed to be speaking in English,' he told him. 'Remember?'

'So? Papa can't hear us. As long as we remember to speak English in front of him, we're fine.'

Louis hugged his knees. 'Do you think we're going to stay with this woman all week?'

'I guess so. She's obviously an old friend of Papa's.'

Louis shot Max a look. 'D'you think she's his new girlfriend?'

'I'm guessing more like an ex-girlfriend. She said in

the car that she hadn't seen him for years. And when we were downstairs, she mentioned something about her divorce. And there's something about the way she looks at him . . .'

'D'you think they're getting married? D'you think that's why we're here?'

'No, stupid. Maybe that's what she's hoping, but Papa would have told us if he was planning on doing something important like that.'

'I wouldn't be so sure,' Louis muttered.

Max raised himself on one arm. 'Why are you so annoyed with Papa anyway?'

Louis struggled to come up with an acceptable reason. 'I just think he should have told us he was taking us on holiday for a week. I could have told Pierre I wouldn't be able to come over, and told my dance teacher I couldn't make the Rouen competition . . .'

Max flopped back against the pillow. 'God, I can't believe you're thinking about your dance class while we're on holiday. The next thing you'll be doing is asking Papa to buy you a tutu—' He broke off as Louis jumped to his feet and thumped him hard. 'Aargh! I'm kidding, I'm kidding—'

'You think you're so funny!' Louis shot him a disgusted look and stalked out. The sound of Max's laughter followed him out onto the landing. But there he stopped. Downstairs, in the kitchen, he could hear the steady rise and fall of Dad's voice. He didn't want to have to go down and make polite conversation with Dad's friend again. Above him, Millie's feet pitter-pattered across the floor of the attic – no doubt she was having a whale of a time arranging all her stuff. The door of the room next door to theirs was closed – Meg's bedroom presumably – and the door at the end of the landing was ajar. He pushed it open, and found to his relief that it was a bathroom.

After going to the loo, he sat down on the closed lid and stared out of the small casement window. Through the branches of a tree, he could see down into Meg's front yard and across the street at the row of houses on the other side. Just as in Ireland, none of the windows here had shutters. Louis wished he felt happier about this holiday. What was wrong with him? Usually he loved taking the plane, flying off to another country – for example, a year and a half ago when Dad had taken them skiing in Switzerland, or the summer before that when they had gone to visit Grandma and Granddad in Cork. OK, so this time he knew something that his brother and sister didn't – a bombshell that Dad would be forced to deliver before the end of the week – but his father had promised he would fight the decision, hadn't he? He would never accept this once-a-month-supervised-visit thing – he would go back to the court and appeal, and would succeed in getting the decision overturned. But if he didn't . . . ? What if he didn't? Suddenly, Louis felt angry. It wasn't fair of Dad to have made him promise not to tell the others. It wasn't fair that he was stuck with that awful thought, hanging over him like a dark cloud for the rest of the week, while Max and Millie had a carefree holiday . . . But a small voice inside his head said, 'And who forced you to eavesdrop?'

Millie burst into the bathroom, making him jump. So the bolt on the door didn't even work properly – *great*.

She padded in barefoot, a Barbie in each hand, went over to the washbasin and began filling it with water. 'What are you doing, Louis?'

'Nothing. Thinking.'

'Did you have a fight with Max?'

'No. Kind of. What are you doing to those poor dolls now?'

'Giving them a bath,' Millie said, as if stating the obvious. 'D'you want to help me?'

'No *thank* you!'

'You never play dolls with me any more,' Millie complained.

Louis glared at her. 'I never *ever* played dolls with you—'

Millie started to giggle.

'Millie, what did I tell you?'

'But none of your school friends are here now,' she protested.

'I said you weren't to tell anyone! That means even me!'

Millie gave a long-suffering sigh. 'I wish I had a sister,' she said.

'And I wish I was an only child,' Louis snapped back.

Undeterred by her brother's foul mood, Millie began pumping large quantities of Meg's apricot-scented hand-wash into the basin and mixing it around to make bubbles. 'Mm, look at this, Sara and Lucie, it's a jacuzzi,' she informed her dolls.

'Have you asked Papa's friend whether you could make a jacuzzi in her sink?' Louis asked her.

'No, Meg and Papa are still in the kitchen, talking,' Millie complained, dipping the first plastic doll into the water. 'I went downstairs but they were almost whispering, and then Papa told me to go and unpack.'

'Great. So we *are* staying here all week.'

Millie turned from her doll-bath to look at him. 'Why? Don't you like it here?'

'We don't even know her,' Louis said grumpily.

Millie turned back to the basin. 'You're always in a bad mood when we have to meet new people.'

'Am not.'

'Yes you are. Papa says it's because you're shy. Except when you're dancing. Then you want everybody to look at you.'

'Do not!'

'Yes you do. When you start doing your spins and backward walkovers and body-popping stuff, *everyone* looks at you, even Maman. It's not fair.'

After a dinner of spaghetti bolognese, they watched two DVDs back-to-back in the lounge while Meg and Dad stayed in the kitchen to do the washing up, then Dad suggested they all have yet another early night. This time no one protested. Having been up since five, even Max looked exhausted.

'And tomorrow? What are we going to do tomorrow?' Millie demanded excitedly, jumping up and down.

'Er – well, we'll see,' Dad answered vaguely.

But although Louis was thankful that the day was over, he found it impossible to sleep in the sagging, creaky bed, and soon began to toss and turn, unable to find a position that was bearable for more than a few seconds. Max fell asleep almost immediately, which irritated him all the more.

The next morning, Louis woke late, the sun already high in the sky. Max's bed was empty, and when he padded out onto the landing, he could hear the sound of voices in the kitchen below. He had a quick shower, pulled on a clean pair of jeans and a T-shirt, and braced himself before stepping into the kitchen. Dad was not there, and Meg was at the cooker frying eggs and bacon in a pan; Max and Millie were seated at the table, chatting noisily.

'Good morning, Louis!' Meg greeted him. 'Did you sleep well?'

Louis mumbled good morning and slid into a chair beside Max.

Breakfast was torturous. Meg served him bacon and eggs, which he could barely swallow. There was no hot chocolate, no proper bread – only sliced brown stuff that tasted like cardboard. Max and Millie seemed delighted by their greasy breakfast and ate masses. Meg asked them about school, about their friends, about life in France, and Max and Millie didn't stop talking, delighted to have such a captive audience. Finally, Louis put down his fork and said, 'Where's Papa?'

'Your dad's gone to sort out some things this

morning,' Meg replied, 'but he said he'd be back before lunch.'

They spent the rest of the morning watching DVDs. Meg went out to the rental shop to get them the films they wanted, but she wouldn't let them come too. Millie played with the cat in the garden and it seemed like ages before Dad came back, but when he did, he was smiling.

'All sorted?' Meg asked, flashing him a knowing look.

'All sorted,' Dad replied. 'Come outside, everyone. I've got something to show you.'

They traipsed out after him into the street. Parked in front of the house was a car – a large blue car with several dents and a chipped front light. But it had a wide back seat and a vast boot.

'Wow!' Max exclaimed. 'What make is it?'

'A Peugeot,' Dad replied, looking pleased with himself. 'It's got a low mileage and apart from the bodywork, it's in good shape. Shall we give it a spin?'

'Yes please, yes please!' Millie cried.

They all piled in, Meg in the front and the three of them in the back, and went for a drive around London, and saw the Houses of Parliament, Big Ben, the London Eye, Buckingham Palace – although Dad wouldn't let them out of the car. On their way back they picked up a Chinese takeaway for lunch, and everyone seemed in really high spirits until Meg suddenly said, 'Millie, I'd really like to cut your hair.'

They were all seated round the kitchen table, finishing the last of the egg fried rice, and Millie put down her spoon and her eyes grew wide. 'Why?' she asked, her voice shrill with outrage.

'Because it's really very pretty, but I think it would suit you better if it was a bit shorter. Like in a bob, for instance.'

'What's a bob?' Millie wanted to know.

Meg demonstrated on her own hair.

'Ew, that's like a boy's,' Millie protested.

'You know, Meg used to be a hairdresser,' Dad chipped in. 'I'm sure she would make it look really lovely, Millie.'

Millie looked reluctant. 'But it's taken me ages and ages to grow it this long. I've got the longest hair in the whole class!'

'But long hair is hot and uncomfortable in the summer. And your hair could be so pretty. If I gave you a bob it would be even curlier and would frame your face and make you look like a little pixie!'

Millie hesitated, clearly torn between pleasing Dad's friend and keeping her long hair.

'Then when we've done that we could go out and buy

you some butterfly clips which would look really nice in short hair,' Meg said.

That did it. 'OK.' Millie glanced shyly at Dad for approval. He beamed.

While Millie and Meg were in the upstairs bathroom, Dad turned to Louis and Max. 'That's put me in the mood for a bit of a shake-up!' he declared suddenly. 'Why don't we all smarten ourselves up a bit? I think I'll get rid of my moustache. Max, why don't I take you to the optician's for those contact lenses I've been promising you?'

Max's face lit up. 'Really?'

'Yes, and your hair could do with a cut too.'

'I want to have a brush cut,' Max said. 'But Maman won't let me.'

'Well, now's the time!'

Max looked worried. 'She'll kill me . . .'

'I'll tell her I made you do it! Come on, let's see what Meg thinks. Louis? Fancy a brush cut?'

'No way,' Louis said.

'Come on! If we're all having haircuts, you've got to do something as well,' Dad persisted. 'How about a different colour then? Brown?'

Louis stared at him. 'Are you crazy?'

'Let Meg give you a trim at least. Your hair really

is too long, Louis. You're beginning to look like a girl.'

Louis gaped at him, hurt, but Dad just smiled. 'Come on then, Max. Let's go to the optician's.'

'Cool!' Max exclaimed.

They left Louis sitting at the table and banged out of the house. Louis sat among the dirty plates and empty plastic containers and rested his chin on his hands. He knew he was being a spoilsport but he just couldn't get his head around this sudden change in Dad. The last-minute surprise holiday, disappearing for hours without them, the close friend they knew nothing about, and now this. Was he trying to seriously anger Maman? Yes, that must be it: *Try and take my children away from me and I will get them to do all the things you've forbidden*. Now Max would probably come back with an earring.

Max didn't come back with an earring, but did come home wearing brown contact lenses, and after a very short crew cut from Meg, his hair seemed to have turned brown too, and he was barely recognizable. True to her word, Meg went out with Millie and bought her a huge assortment of butterfly clips, which pleased Millie no end – and the bob did suit her. Louis had no choice but to let Meg 'trim' his hair, but she ended up cutting it much shorter than she said she would, into a spiky modern style that Louis instantly hated. Dad shaved off his moustache and Meg gave him a crew cut too, and then he dyed his greying hair brown and everyone agreed that he looked ten years younger. Then it was time for dinner and Dad made pancakes and cracked jokes and suddenly appeared to be in the best mood he had been in for days.

But the next day he woke them up at half past five in the morning and told them to hurry and get dressed. They were going on the last lap of their journey.

Chapter Four

They had been driving for hours. Max was in the front seat, trainers up on the dashboard, music blaring in his earphones. Millie was asleep, her head lolling against the strap of her seatbelt, her short hair curling across her cheek. There had scarcely been time to say goodbye to Meg – Dad had bundled them into the car while she had stood in her dressing gown, blinking in the doorway. But before getting into the driver's seat, Dad had hugged her hard and whispered, 'Thank you. Thank you so much.' Now it was almost eight in the morning and a pale, watery dawn had broken through the clouds above them. They had long since left London behind, and the rows of terraced houses had been replaced by rolling fields dotted with sheep, the motorway stretching out in front of them, bleak, grey and endless.

Fiddling with his watch, Louis suddenly noticed it was Tuesday. He was startled. Somehow he had thought it was still the weekend, albeit a very long one, and he was taken aback to realize he had already missed a whole day of school. Pierre would be wondering where on earth he was, especially if he had rung Dad's flat at the weekend and got no answer. Then again, Pierre would probably have rung the house and got onto Maman by now, and she would have explained everything to him. England was an hour behind France, so right now Maman would be on her way to work; Pierre would be arriving at school, no doubt envying Louis his sudden holiday. Tuesdays were a bummer. They had double maths in the morning, followed by physics and chemistry and then a long coach ride and an afternoon of horrible swimming in a chlorine-stenched pool. Nonetheless, Tuesdays remained his favourite day of the week, because after school he had his street-dance class.

Millie stirred and opened her eyes and then sat up with a start, looking around wildly. Then she seemed to remember where she was, for she sat back against the seat, blinking sleepily. 'Papa – Daddy – I need to go to the loo,' she said.

He glanced down at his watch. 'OK, we'll stop for breakfast at the next exit.'

When they got out of the car, they were met by a chill wind and a splattering of rain. Louis' muscles felt cramped, there was a stale taste in his mouth and his head felt foggy. They walked across the windy car park to the toilets and then into a large, bright, noisy food hall. Dad let them have whatever they wanted so they all ordered burgers and chips and tucked in hungrily. Dad ordered a ham sandwich but ate less than half of it.

'How much further?' Max asked.

'Another two hundred miles or so.'

'What's that in kilometres?' Max persisted.

'What's that in hours?' Millie added.

Dad rubbed his eyes, looking tired. 'Three hours, if we're lucky,' he said.

Millie gasped dramatically.

'So where are we going then?' Louis asked. 'Surely you can tell us now.'

Dad sighed. 'You'll see when we get there, Louis.'

Max rolled his eyes. It seemed he was tiring of this surprise thing too.

After breakfast, when Dad suggested they get back in the car and 'press on' with the journey, he met with howls of protest.

'All right, all right,' he said quickly. 'Let's go for a wander and stretch our legs.'

At the end of the car park was a long strip of grass overlooking the motorway. Millie went skipping down it, looking for daisies. Max found a partially deflated football and kicked it over to Louis. They began a makeshift game, using their jackets as goalposts, and even managed to persuade Dad to join in.

'Not fair! Whose side are you on?' Louis shouted as Dad kicked the ball between his goalposts.

'I'll have to be the third team,' Dad said, laughing.

'No, wait,' Max said. 'We'll get Millie. Then it can be two against two. Millie!' he shouted.

'Bags me be with Dad,' Louis said quickly.

'No way! Millie has to be with Dad – Dad's too good!' Max protested.

'I'm flattered,' Dad said, practising his goal-scoring.

'Millie!' Max yelled. 'Come and play!'

'I'm busy! I'm making a daisy chain!' she called back.

'You can be on Dad's team!' Max shouted.

She hesitated for a moment, then put down the daisy chain and came running over. 'But you have to let me get the ball, you have to let me get the ball!'

They started the game, Max and Louis against Dad and Millie. Dad got stuck in, and despite her size, Millie was like a bullet, accustomed to being roped into games of football with her older brothers. Louis felt chuffed that Max had wanted him on his team and the two of them did their best to outplay Dad and Millie, who were both prone to bending the rules. Millie liked to engage in rugby-type tackles, throwing herself round the legs of her opponent and knocking him to the ground, and at one point there was a real rugby scrum, with them all piling on top of Dad. When they were too out of breath to run any more, they decided to have a penalty shoot-out. Louis went in goal, and while Dad and Millie were arguing over who was going to take the ball, he did a couple of backflips. He felt happier than he had in days. Perhaps this holiday was going to be a success after all.

Back in the car, Millie soon fell asleep again, grazes and grass stains covering her elbows and knees. Dad had the French radio on very low and Max was plugged into his iPod again . . .

After a while Louis realized he must have dozed off, because quite suddenly the sun was high, blazing down from a massive stretch of blue sky. He sat up groggily to look out of the window and saw that they were surrounded by the most extraordinary scenery – green and brown mountains and, in the distance, the shimmering water of a vast lake.

'Where are we?' he asked Dad.

'This is the Lake District,' Dad replied. 'Isn't it beautiful?'

'Yes,' Louis replied. He could scarcely believe they were still in England. 'Is this where we're going to be staying?'

'Yes,' Dad replied.

'With another one of your friends?'

'No, we're renting a little farmhouse,' Dad said. 'It'll just be the four of us.'

Louis smiled.

Sometime later, they turned off the road and onto a long bumpy dirt track that snaked its way across rough grassy hillside towards a small farmhouse, set half a mile back from the road. As they approached it in the juddering car, Louis saw that it was two storeys high, built of grey stone with a slate roof.

'The house is a hundred years old,' Dad explained, finally switching off the engine and getting out of the car. He took a deep breath and gazed around. 'These two acres of land belong to it. Crikey, just look at all this space.'

As they followed him out, the air was very still, broken only by the faint twitter of birdsong. Max dug his hands into his jeans pockets and gave a low whistle.

75

'Wow,' Millie breathed softly. 'Beautiful.'

Behind the farmhouse, the grassland rose gradually towards a towering peak. On the other side, several miles away, more green peaks pointed up towards a brilliant blue sky. Below them, a huge, inky-blue lake stretched out like a sheet of glass. A cluster of houses in the distance suggested a village. A cool wind lifted Louis' hair and stroked his bare arms. He shivered. They had arrived in the middle of nowhere.

They quickly began to explore the premises, Millie running about in excitement. To the left of the house, a corrugated-iron door led to a vast barn, empty save for a few bales of hay and some bits of broken machinery. Inside the farmhouse, the small kitchen was dark and damp, all the surfaces were covered with dust, and there was an evil smell coming from the fridge. The narrow corridor was dark and cold and the brown carpet was in dire need of vacuuming. The living room was not much better: an old, disused fireplace and a sagging brown couch. A steep flight of stairs led up to a manky green bathroom with cracked tiles; then came a small study, followed by two decent-sized bedrooms, one containing a single bed, the other a double.

'So I don't get my own room,' Millie realized, doing the maths.

Max shrugged, clearly unimpressed by the inside of the house. 'Looks like only one of us gets their own *bed*.'

There was the sound of Dad's feet on the stairs and he appeared, slightly breathless, carrying some bags. 'Now don't look so disheartened. The house has potential. We'll just need to buy a few things, that's all.'

'But we're only staying here for four days,' Louis said. 'What's the point?'

'The point is' – Dad took a deep breath – 'I want my children to be comfortable. Now, who's got a pen and paper . . . ?' He rummaged in Millie's rucksack. 'Let's make a list.'

'Oh, can I do it? Can I do it?' Millie grabbed the pen and paper from Dad's hand. List-making was one of her passions.

'OK.' Dad sat down on the sagging mattress. 'Let's just start with the basics. We need cleaning products to get rid of all this dust. I think there's a vacuum cleaner in the closet downstairs but I'll need to check it works. Bed sheets – one double, one single. Pillows, one each – that's four. Four pillowcases. One double duvet and duvet cover. Three single duvets and duvet covers.'

'Why?' Max asked. 'We've only got two beds.'

'Hold on, hold on,' Dad said. 'I'm just getting to that. Now, we'll need two single beds—'

'Two beds!' Millie began to laugh. 'We can't buy beds, Daddy!'

'Yes we can,' Dad said quickly. 'Meg has asked me to do the place up for her.' His eyes shifted uncomfortably.

'This is Meg's place?' Max wanted to know.

'Her holiday home. Yes. Now, let's move on . . .'

An unsteady feeling started in the pit of Louis' stomach again. If Papa had rented a farmhouse for four days, why hadn't he gone through a travel agency and got a place that was clean and already contained enough beds? It didn't make sense. Beds took time to be delivered, and by the time they arrived, they would probably be on their way back to France.

'We'll also need some kind of mattresses to tide us over till the beds come,' Dad said. 'Right, let's go down to the kitchen and see what's needed there.'

They spent the rest of the day in a crazy whirl. Dad really seemed to be taking the task to heart, for he set them all a list of jobs while he disappeared with the car. On his hands and knees, scrubbing out the stinking fridge with Brillo pads, Louis wondered what on earth was going on. In the corridor, Max was vacuuming the carpet, and in the living room, Millie was wiping down all the surfaces. It was as if Dad was planning to live here permanently. All of a sudden, the thought stopped him. That was it! Dad was planning to move to England! He was going to rent the house from Meg and wanted them all to help out with getting it habitable. He was buying them beds because he was planning to have them all come and stay with him during the holidays while Maman was still working. That must be it! But he needed to get the house into tip-top shape if he was ever to persuade Maman to let them visit. So what about the court case? Well, perhaps Maman had already backed down. Perhaps Maman had said, *Fine, you can have the kids to stay, but only if you move out of that tiny flat in Paris and get something decent.* And so that was what Dad was doing!

Dropping the Brillo pad, Louis jumped up to share the news with Max and Millie, leaving out the bit about the court case. They were as excited as he was, but Max suddenly said, 'Hold on. Why then all the secrecy? Wouldn't he have just come out with the plan and told us about it right from the start?'

'Maybe he wanted to surprise us,' Louis said. 'Or maybe he doesn't want Maman to know yet.'

'D'you think she'll let us come here every weekend?' Millie crowed happily.

'Not every weekend, it would be too expensive,' Max

told her. 'But perhaps for the school holidays, instead of paying for that stupid summer camp.'

'But I don't want to just see Papa in the school holidays!' Millie complained. 'And I don't want Papa to move to England!' Her bottom lip wobbled ominously.

'Let's just wait and see,' Louis said quickly. 'Dad will have to tell us soon. And maybe it's just a holiday home for him too. We don't know yet.'

They went back to their respective tasks. An hour later, things were already beginning to look better. Louis' back was killing him, but the fridge no longer smelled, the kitchen surfaces were clean and the floor was washed. Max had progressed to vacuuming the bedrooms and Millie had finished the dusting and moved on to scrubbing the bathroom. Louis threw open all the windows to get rid of the musty smell, and when Dad came in, there was a mini gale buffeting through the house.

They went out to help unload the car: the vast boot was full of things, from saucepan scourers to dishcloths, from pillows to doormats. Max cut the price tags off everything and Louis and Millie went to make the beds. Then Dad got to work with a hammer, smashing up the large, cumbersome desk in the study to turn it into Millie's room.

That evening everyone was shattered, and they went to bed after eggs on toast, with Dad promising to take them into town to explore and do some more shopping the next day. Louis and Max flipped a coin for the single bed in their bedroom and Louis won, so Max got the mattress on the floor. In the ex-study, Millie found a spider, which produced much hysteria and resulted in her sharing the double bed with Dad. But as soon as Louis' head hit the new pillow, he fell fast asleep.

Straight after breakfast the next morning, they got in the car and drove into town. Now that they were calling the farmhouse 'Dad's new holiday home' he seemed to have relaxed a bit about it and was no longer being quite so cryptic. It was fun, furnishing a new home, and Max and Millie made long lists of all the things they thought he needed. Max's list mainly involved electrical equipment – from computers to PlayStations to Xboxes. Millie's list included a pet cat. Dad laughed as he drove and told them to go easy.

In the end they got a portable television with an inbuilt DVD player, a wooden dolls' house that Millie almost collapsed over, two beds placed on order, and a washer-dryer. They walked around Kendal, sat on a bench and ate a strange meal of fried fish with chips, and then Dad took them to a bike shop and told them they could choose any bike they wanted. They were in seventh heaven. They hadn't been allowed to have bikes back in Paris because the roads were too dangerous. Around the tiny village of Grasmere, it seemed, there were very few main roads, but lots of long, smooth paths weaving around the lakes and in and out of the valley. Millie found a pink bike with a wicker basket that seduced her almost instantly. Louis chose a robust-looking mountain bike with eighteen gears. Max took ages choosing his bike, reading all the literature available, going through the different gears and speeds and makes with the very obliging shopkeeper until they were all ready to throttle him. But when they were just about to leave, a strange thing happened. The shopkeeper asked them where they were all from and Millie had just started to say 'Paris' when Dad interrupted her with 'New Caledonia'.

'Oh, that's a lovely part of the world,' the shopkeeper began. 'We have relatives over there who—'

'Do excuse us but we must really get going,' Dad said, ushering them all out of the shop.

Outside, Max was laughing at Dad. 'Why did you tell that old man we came from New Caledonia?' he asked.

'I didn't like him,' Dad said quickly. 'I didn't like the way he was looking at you. I think there was something funny about him. I didn't want him to know where we were from.'

'But he seemed really nice!' Millie protested.

Dad suddenly pointed out that because he hadn't got a roof rack for the Peugeot yet, Max and Louis would have to cycle home. 'I'll drive as slowly as I can and you can follow the car,' he said.

But Max had a better idea. 'We can go and explore!'

'You'll get lost,' Dad said.

'No we won't. I remember the way back – it's not exactly far,' Max retorted.

Dad looked reluctant but, after a moment's hesitation, gave in. He unfolded his map over the bonnet of the car and talked them through the five-mile route home. Millie protested that she wanted to come too but Dad distracted her with talk of going home to erect her dolls' house. With last-minute warnings echoing in their ears, Max and Louis cycled off.

As they came out of the town, Louis spotted a pay phone on a street corner and skidded to a halt.

'What are you doing?' Max demanded, slowing down reluctantly.

Louis dug his hand into the pocket of his jeans for the change Dad had let him keep when he'd paid for the bike.

'I'm gonna call Pierre. Tell him I've gone on holiday. He'll be so jealous!'

'You don't know the international dialling code—'

'Yes I do.'

'Fine. Then catch me up,' Max said, turning his bike round and disappearing down the winding road.

It took several seconds for the long beeps to sound. As soon as Pierre answered, a row of zeros began flashing on the display, the phone demanding to be fed again.

'*Ouais*?' Pierre's voice sounded very distant.

'It's Louis – guess where I am?'

'What's going on? Where are you?'

'England! Papa took us on holiday. We're in a place called the Lake District, it's really cool, I'm not coming back to school till Monday—'

A series of loud beeps muffled the sound of Pierre's voice. Then the line went dead. Louis hung up, disgusted that the phone had swallowed up a whole pound in a matter of seconds. Then he straddled his bike again, pumping the pedals furiously to catch up with Max.

The late-afternoon sun was beginning to turn golden and touch the tops of the trees. They left the town behind them and Max set the pace, taking a winding road that led down towards the lake. It stretched out like a vast sheet of turquoise glass, the warm sun giving it a golden hue. Dramatic peaks towered all around them beneath a vast white sky. The wind blew strong, whipping tears from their eyes. Louis stood up on his pedals, looking out across the water. Ahead of him, Max skidded to a halt on the stony verge, threw his bike down on the grass and looked down at the jagged hillside. 'Reckon we could climb down there?'

Louis laid his bike down and tested the ground with his foot. It felt reasonably firm. 'Don't see why not.'

They began their descent, turning sideways and digging the edges of their trainers into the earth, using their hands to stay balanced, and for a while the only sound was the scrabbling of feet and the rasping of breath, until Louis reached the bottom first and splodged through the wet mud at the edge of the lake. Moments later, Max followed him, and the two of them stood looking out across the vast expanse of water. The wind had dropped, and apart from the lazy chirping of a swallow, the air was eerily still.

Max bent down to look for stones, his cheeks flushed pink from their hasty descent. He found some flattish ones and began skimming them one by one across the water.

Louis picked up a stone and tried to skim it too, but it only disappeared with an irritating plop. 'Why can't I do it?'

'You need to get flat ones, like this.' Max handed him

a stone. 'Then imagine you're throwing a tiny little frisbee. Like this . . .' The stone skimmed the water three times.

Louis tried, with a disappointing result. 'Pfff.'

'Nearly,' Max said. 'Try again. But turn your hand inwards when you throw, like this.' He demonstrated.

Louis tried again. A sort of half-skim, before the stone disappeared again.

'Better,' Max said encouragingly.

Louis bent down to look for some more flat stones as Max skimmed another across the ripples.

Louis had another go. This time there was a definite skim. 'Whoa!' he exclaimed.

Max threw another stone and said, 'So what d'you think about the farmhouse?'

Louis glanced at him. 'It's a bit run down but I like it.'

There was a pause. Then Max suddenly said, 'Dad's not coming back to France – you know that, don't you.'

Louis felt his heart judder. He looked sharply at Max. 'How d'you know?'

'It's obvious,' Max said, sounding as if he didn't really care. 'Dad might have savings but he's not that rich. He wouldn't be going to all this trouble to furnish the house if he was only going to use it for the holidays.'

'You mean you think he's going to live here?'

'Of course,' Max said.

Louis felt his eyes narrow. 'You don't know that,' he tried.

Max shot him an exasperated look. 'Oh, come *on*.'

'OK,' Louis reluctantly agreed. 'So maybe he is planning to stay here for a bit. That doesn't mean he'll never come back to France. And it'll mean *we* get to spend all our holidays *here*. Heaps better than horrid summer camp, if you ask me.'

Max looked at him darkly, his hands dug deep in his pockets. 'You really think Maman's going to let us fly out to England and spend the holidays with Dad?'

Louis could feel his chin jutting out defensively. 'She might—'

'Oh, *come on*!' Max exclaimed angrily. 'She doesn't even want us to spend a weekend with him once a month in Paris!'

Louis threw a stone as hard as he could. It skimmed the water three times. He didn't want to look at Max. 'So what are you saying?'

'What I'm saying is – Dad must have lost the court case.'

A sliver of shock shot through Louis' stomach. He threw another stone.

There was a long silence. Max stared at Louis' face. Then, 'Oh my God, you knew,' he breathed.

Louis scrabbled around for more stones. 'I don't know what you're talking about—'

'Oh my God, you *knew*!' Suddenly Louis felt himself shoved backwards and slammed down against the hard ground, Max's fingers twisting the collar of his T-shirt, his fist against Louis' throat.

'Tell me everything, right now, or I'll swear I'll punch you—'

'OK, OK!' Louis held up his hands. He had never seen Max so angry. For the first time in his life, Louis actually felt afraid of his older brother.

With a furious shove, Max let go of Louis' collar and Louis sat up, breathing hard. 'Jesus, Max, there's no need to—'

'You tell me everything, right now, or I swear to God . . .' Max's eyes were flashing, the colour high in his cheeks.

'You've got to promise not to tell Millie. Dad made me promise not to tell either of you, and—'

'OK, OK!'

Louis took a deep, shuddering breath. The sun had disappeared behind a cloud. 'You guessed right,' he said in a rush. 'Dad lost the court case and Mum won. He's only allowed supervised visits with us from now on. But he's going to—'

Max had grabbed him by the collar again. 'How do you know? Who told you?'

'I overheard Dad on the phone!'

'When?'

'The night before we left!'

Max whistled under his breath, slowly remembering. 'So that's when you . . . when we were playing Cluedo, and you came out of the kitchen and you'd been crying—'

'I wasn't crying,' Louis said quickly, but Max didn't appear to hear him. His face darkened.

'So that's why Dad's moving to England? Because he lost the court case?'

'I don't know,' Louis said. 'It doesn't make sense. He said he was going to appeal. He promised, Max! Maybe the farmhouse really *is* just a holiday home. Maybe he wants to do it up so he can prove to Mum that he's not ill any more and she'll trust him to look after us . . .'

But Max was looking away, shaking his head in disgust. 'Don't be so bloody naïve. He won't be appealing if he's moving to England. He must just be hoping to start his life over and meet some new woman—'

'You don't know that!' Louis felt his voice rising. 'He wouldn't do that! He would never give us up! He promised me – he said everything was going to be all right!'

'Those are just words,' Max scoffed. 'You were blubbing like a baby and he just wanted to shut you up—'

Louis jumped to his feet and started to climb back up the hillside towards the bikes.

Max started to follow him. 'Hey, Louis, I'm sorry. Come on, calm down.'

Louis ignored him and kept on going, digging his nails into the soft earth to aid his ascent, the growing burn in his calf muscles a useful antidote to the pain inside his mind.

The next day, the beds arrived, and Louis and Millie helped Dad erect them in the bedrooms. They did Millie's first, and when it was done, she was so pleased with it that she turned somersaults on the fresh bouncy mattress.

'I want to paint my walls pink,' she declared, stretching out over her Barbie duvet cover.

'I think that could be arranged,' Dad replied.

'Really? Oh, yippee! I want to call Maman and tell her about my new room. Can I call her now, Daddy?'

Dad appeared not to have heard; he was collecting up his tools, ready to move on to the next room.

'Can I call *Mummy*?' Millie repeated, appearing to

think her use of the French word was the reason Dad hadn't replied.

Dad picked up his toolbox and went next door to the boys' room. Louis followed him, Millie skipping behind. 'Can I, Daddy, can I, can I?'

Dad put down his toolbox on Louis' bed, the colour high in his cheeks. 'Not now, Millie, she'll be at work.'

'But Mummy's always at work. She lets me call her at work – I'm allowed.'

'Only if it's for something important,' Louis reminded her.

'But this *is* important. I want to tell her about my new room! Oh please, Daddy!'

'We can't call her yet, we haven't got a phone installed,' Dad told her.

'But on your mobile—'

'No, Millie, it's too expensive.' The tone of Dad's voice signalled that the discussion was over.

For a moment Millie looked upset, hurt even. Then she quickly recovered, remembering her new bed, and ran back to her room.

Louis and Dad got to work on the second bed, Louis cutting open the cardboard boxes while Dad pored over the instructions. Louis lined up the wooden panels according to size and knelt on the carpet opposite his father, following his lead with the first set of screws. Louis used the electric screwdriver while Dad took the manual one, and once the screws were in place, they returned to the instruction leaflet, studying it together.

'I think we have to hammer in the dowels next,' Louis said, picking up the handful of wooden pegs.

'OK, you do that while I screw the bolts into the blocks,' Dad replied. 'Where's the electric screwdriver?'

'Here. Can you pass me the hammer?'

'Here.'

For several minutes they worked in silence, the pounding of the hammer filling the air. When Louis sat back and looked critically at his handiwork, Dad glanced over and said, 'Good job. You've got them in nice and deep.'

'D'you want a hand with the bolts?' Louis asked him.

'Yes please.'

Louis picked up the manual screwdriver and got stuck in. There was another silence. Then Dad said, 'Louis, do you like it here?'

The screwdriver slipped sharply away from the bolt. Louis swore. He put the tip back into place and raised himself on his knees for leverage. A moment passed. 'Yeah.'

'*Really* like it? More than Paris?'

'It's different,' Louis said.

'But where would you prefer to live? If you had the choice, I mean.' Dad was sitting back on his heels, watching Louis carefully.

Louis picked up the discarded electric screwdriver. 'Can I use this then?'

'Go ahead.' Another moment. 'Louis?'

'Mm.'

'You haven't answered my question.'

'I don't know.' Louis narrowed his eyes in concentration and watched the screw whirr noisily into the wood. 'Is that in far enough?'

'That's fine . . . I mean, if you had the choice. Would you prefer to live in a big city like Paris or out in the countryside somewhere like this?'

'Both,' Louis said.

'Both?' It clearly wasn't the answer Dad was expecting.

'Yeah, term time in Paris, and then holidays here in England.' Louis leaned forward to look at the instruction sheet. 'OK, so now we have to position the slats between the side rails. Look, we're almost done!'

Chapter Five

Saturday seemed to creep up on them completely un-expectedly; they were sitting around the breakfast table amidst the crumbs and the croissants and the pots of jam when Millie caught sight of the date on Dad's newspaper and suddenly declared, 'We're going home tomorrow.'

There was a silence and Louis exchanged glances with Max and Millie. He knew what they were thinking. It still felt like they had just arrived: the farmhouse was only beginning to feel comfortable and their bedrooms like proper bedrooms. It seemed crazy that they had gone to all this trouble making the place nice, only to have to leave it again. And who knew when, if ever, they would be allowed to come back? If Maman had her way . . .

Millie stretched her arm across the table to rustle

Dad's newspaper. 'Oh, Dad, please can we stay . . .?' she said, in a voice that had already accepted defeat but wanted to have a go anyway.

'Yeah,' Max chipped in. 'School breaks up in three weeks. Can't we just stay here for the summer?'

Dad glanced up sharply. 'Would you like to?'

Max looked taken aback. 'What?'

'Stay,' Dad said. 'I dunno – an extra week perhaps . . .'

'Really?' Millie clapped her hands, her eyes bright.

'Are you serious, Dad?' Max looked disbelieving.

Dad shrugged. 'Why not? Missing the last bit of school won't hurt—'

'We can't,' Louis said.

They all looked at him. 'Why not?'

'Because . . .' He floundered for a moment. 'Because we still have school, Max. I have two tests next week, and if I miss them I'll get zero. And because you have football practice and Millie has art club and I have dance classes and I can't miss them two weeks in a row—'

'Oh, I might have guessed!' Max rolled his eyes dramatically. 'This is just because you're worried if you miss your precious *ballet* lesson you won't be top of the class any more—'

'It's got nothing to do with that!' Louis suddenly

shouted. 'You know very well that Maman's not going to let us stay here for another whole week!'

'Stop being such a baby!'

'It's called being realistic!'

'OK, calm down, everyone,' Dad said, folding the paper. 'Let me speak to Mum and see what she says. I'm sure your teacher will understand if I write you a note, Louis. And wouldn't it be good to spend a few more days in the farmhouse now that we've worked so hard at getting it nice?'

'Oh yay!' Millie cried. 'Thank you, Daddy, thank you, Daddy, thank you, Daddy!'

Max shot Louis a look across the table. It was a look that said, *Don't you even* dare *try and protest*. And Louis felt that strange feeling in the pit of his stomach. The feeling that something wasn't right.

That afternoon they had a very windy lakeside picnic and then Dad hired a bike from the village shop and they all went cycling. On the way home they picked up some DVDs and ate pizza in the living room in front of the TV. Halfway through the film, Dad came in, a big smile on his face. 'I've spoken to Mum and managed to persuade her. She's going to let the school know and so we're all set for another week.'

Millie turned round with her mouth open. 'Is Maman on the phone? I want to speak to her!'

'Not now, Millie,' Dad replied. 'She's very busy at the moment.'

That night, after Dad had sent them upstairs, Max lay fully clothed on his bed, playing with his GameBoy, while Louis kicked off his jeans and tried to throw them into the hamper on the other side of the room. Max suddenly said, 'Why are you being so funny about staying here another week? Don't you like this place or something?' He didn't look up from his GameBoy, but Louis could tell he wasn't really paying that much attention to the game.

'Of course I like it here,' Louis said, pulling off his socks and sending them the same way as his jeans. 'I just think it's a bit strange, that's all.'

There was a silence. Then Max said, 'Yeah. Me too.'

Louis looked at him sharply, taken by surprise. Well, this *was* a revelation. Could it be that Max was feeling the same sense of unease at the way Dad had spoken to them about extending their holiday? The forced flippancy about missing school; the way his eyes had shied away . . . ?

'What d'you mean?' Louis asked, cross-legged on his bed in his pants and T-shirt, looking at Max carefully. 'I thought you really wanted to stay.'

'I did.' Max still didn't look up. 'I wanted Dad to try and persuade Mum to let us stay, just on the off chance that he might be successful. But I never thought it would work.'

'You mean you wanted to stay in theory, but when it became a reality, you realized you'd rather go home?'

'Are you kidding me? Go back to school and tests and screaming teachers and all that crap?' Max did look up now, switching off his GameBoy and tossing it across the bed. 'Of course not. I'd much rather stay here.'

'So what are you saying?'

'What I'm saying is . . .' There was a pause. Max seemed to be choosing his words very carefully. 'I don't think Mum agreed to this.'

'*What?*'

'I think Dad just decided himself to stay here another week. I don't think he called her at all. And if he did call her, then my guess is she said "No way" and Dad said "Tough luck, see you in a week." '

Louis could feel his mouth opening in amazement. 'But you know what Mum's like. She'd be furious! She'd come straight over and drag us back!'

'Would she?' Max looked doubtful. 'I mean, yes, sure, she'd be furious. But if she flew over to England, she'd have to take several days off work, and right now she's in the middle of that big Steinberg deal and working practically round the clock—'

'But Dad must know that once we do go home she'll be so angry with him she'll never let us stay with him again!'

Max gave Louis a meaningful look. 'But if Dad knows this is the last time he's allowed to have us to stay anyway . . .'

A slow grin of amusement crossed Louis' face. It did sound like something Dad might do. He would figure – *I've got nothing to lose and my ex-wife hates me anyway, why not keep my kids on holiday with me for an extra week?* Louis inhaled slowly. 'Mum's going to be soooo mad.' Another thought suddenly occurred to him. 'D'you think she's going to be angry with *us*?'

'She can't,' Max said pragmatically. 'We'll say we thought she'd OK'd the extra week. She never has to know we guessed what was going on.'

'But she might anyway,' Louis countered. 'And then she'll stop all our pocket money and ban us from watching TV for a month and get us to do all the housework like the time when we—'

'Who cares?' Max gave a dismissive shrug. 'Even if she does, it'll still be worth an extra week's holiday with Dad, I reckon.'

Louis smiled. 'Yeah, that's true,' he agreed.

* * *

The following week was much better than the first.
There were still some bits and bobs in the house to tidy
up – Dad repaired the broken cupboard doors in the
kitchen and bought them each a desk and chest of
drawers for their rooms. Dad helped Millie paint her
room pale pink, and for three days she slept in his bed.
They went outside into the garden at the back of the
house and Dad cut the grass with a rusty pair of garden
shears while Max hacked away at the overgrown bracken
and Louis and Millie piled all the garden waste into
heavyduty refuse sacks. They collected the rotting
apples for compost and Dad made Millie a vegetable
patch, where she planted seeds bought at the local
garden centre. They went regularly into Kendal as
Dad was reluctant to let them use the shops in the
village, saying, 'They're all so nosy in a place like this.
They'll start asking lots of questions and wonder why
you aren't in school.' He pretty much forbade them to
speak to strangers, and Louis wondered what on
earth he could be afraid of in a quiet place like this. Now
and again, Dad would have to go into town for 'business'.
Louis didn't know what business he could possibly
have to do here but he didn't ask, for he sensed
that, with the new house and everything, Dad was trying

to get himself back on his feet again. Maybe he wanted to have a job lined up by the time they went back to Paris so that he could then say to Mum, 'Look, I can take care of my own kids. Not only have I got a new house but I'm also in a job again.' Louis didn't say anything to the others, but he so hoped this was the case. If Dad managed to hold down a job, then there couldbe no doubt in anybody's mind that he really was cured.

But time was running away from them and soon they found themselves approaching the end of the week again. Louis turned his thoughts back to school, and the stories he would have to tell Pierre and Luc and the others, and even though he felt sad at the thought of leaving the farmhouse behind, he sensed that they would be back. He had a feeling that Dad was about to turn the corner – he couldn't remember seeing him so relaxed and happy since the divorce. And surely Mum would give in and let them go and stay with Dad again, as soon as she got over her anger that they'd stayed on an extra week.

'Who fancies going to the beach today?' Dad asked one morning at breakfast.

They all looked up at him in surprise. As usual, Millie was spreading Nutella thickly over her toast. Max was devouring a bowlful of chocolate-flavoured cereal. Louis was sticking to croissants.

'Where?' Millie asked, turning to look out of the window as if she expected a beach to suddenly appear in the garden.

'Whitehaven,' Dad replied. 'Less than an hour's drive. And just look at the weather today!'

Outside, the sky was a brilliant blue. Golden sunshine splashed through the kitchen window, creating puddles of light on the breakfast table.

'But it's windy,' Millie pointed out. 'It's not hot enough yet.'

'I'm not suggesting we swim,' Dad said. 'Just that we go for a day trip. Have a walk on the beach. A picnic if it's not too cold.'

'Cool!' Millie exclaimed. 'Daddy, will you buy me a kite?'

'Why not,' Daddy said. 'Max? Louis?'

'Bags me sitting in the front,' Max said quickly.

Louis pulled a face at him.

They set off after breakfast. Millie insisted on packing a rucksack full of dolls as well as a towel in case she felt brave enough to paddle. Dad and Louis made pâté sandwiches and they picked up some lemonade on their way through the village. They arrived in the bustling town of

Whitehaven at noon and Dad left them in a supermarket car park while he ran some errands at the bank, then Louis swapped places with Max and map-read until they reached the coast. They parked the car in a lay-by and climbed the steep sand dunes to survey an empty strip of sandy beach that stretched out in both directions for as far as the eye could see.

Max gave a low whistle into the wind. 'Wicked,' he breathed.

Millie had already spotted a beach shop, set back down by the winding road. 'Daddy, Daddy, let's buy a kite, and an ice cream, and buckets and spades!' she cried.

'All right, all right!' Dad laughed. 'And while we're at it we can go and get the picnic bag from the car.'

'I need to get my iPod,' Max said. 'I left it on the back seat.'

They turned and started making their way back down the sand dune. Then Dad looked round and called, 'Louis?'

But Louis could already feel the heels of his feet rising off the rough grass as he tipped forward down the steep dune towards the vast stretch of beach ahead. The sand was soft and powdery and he half skidded, half tumbled to the bottom, pausing only to pull off his trainers and socks before breaking into a run. Almost immediately, the wind seemed to strengthen, whipping the hair back from his head, screaming in his ears and tearing at his eyes. He took in great lungfuls of the cold, salty air and felt the powdery sand firm up beneath his bare feet. It was an incredible feeling. All this beach, all this sea, all this sky, stretching out in every direction. He felt tiny and insignificant in all this vastness; even when he tried to shout, the sound was immediately whipped from his mouth and extinguished. He felt liberated, intoxicated and wildly free.

The bottoms of his jeans were getting soaked as he splashed through freezing shallow pools of water left behind by the retreating tide. The sand grew firmer still, the little bumps left by the waves pummelling the soles of his feet. He skidded to a stop at the water's edge and began to turn *fouettés*, his favourite dance move. His heart thumped as if it was about to burst but he was determined to beat his personal best of twenty-five turns. When he finally allowed himself to stop, collapsing dramatically onto the wet sand, he felt as if he was going to pass out, but it was a wonderful feeling – a feeling of pushing your body to the limit, a feeling he hadn't had since his last dance lesson. He had missed it so much.

When he could finally breathe again, he rolled his

jeans up to his knees and waded out into the sea as far as he could, his feet and ankles throbbing with cold as he stared out at the grey-green water and crashing waves. From holidays in the south of France he remembered only crowded beaches, soft yellow sand and warm blue water. This was different – stark, cold and desolate.

He turned round to wade back onto dry sand and realized how far he had run, the huge dunes now only molehills in the distance. He could also make out three tiny figures, smudges only, making their way out towards him, following his long trail of footprints. It seemed to take them for ever, even though the smallest of the three figures appeared to be running.

Millie got to him first, her cheeks bright pink from the cold. 'Wow, there's no people, there's no people,' she crowed.

Max arrived next, wearing his earphones and beat-boxing into the wind. Dad arrived last, sounding puffed, carrying a bucket and spade and the picnic bag. 'Good grief, we're all going to freeze,' he said. 'Louis, what have you done with your shoes?'

Millie tiptoed to the water's edge and began to squeal. Max ran to join her and pretended to be trying to push her in. Millie's screams strengthened.

'Max, for heaven's sake don't let her fall in the water!' Dad shouted across the wind.

Louis did a string of cartwheels and backflips along the sea edge, the water soaking into the cuffs of his sweatshirt. Max splashed him and Louis splashed him back and soon they were engaged in a water fight.

Dad shouted something about not having any dry clothes to change into, and so to shut him up, Max started organizing a game of sumo wrestling, drawing out the ring in the sand. He then set out the rules, adding that whoever fought Millie had to do so on one leg.

Max and Dad went first, and even though Dad was stronger and heavier, Max was much more agile and kept jumping out of the way and tripping him up, until finally he got Dad to step out of the circle. Against Millie on one foot, he really struggled and came perilously close to the circle edge before finally getting her to step out. But as Louis stepped forward, Max's eyes narrowed and Louis immediately realized Max was going to give it all he'd got. They pounced together, grabbing each other by the shoulders, and tangled for several minutes, their puffs and grunts filling the air. Millie cheered for Louis and so Dad cheered for Max, and for a long moment there was a standoff, their feet raking up the sand. Then Max's superior strength began to show and Louis' feet began creeping back towards the circle's edge. Waiting till the very last minute, when Max was almost sure he'd won, Louis suddenly turned on the ball of one foot and spun himself round, and Max went flying out of the circle with the force of his own push.

Louis fell onto his knees, punching the air in triumph while Max got slowly to his feet, brushing the sand off the front of his jeans. 'Did you just pull some fancy *dance move*?'

And they were off, the game of wrestling turning into a game of tag, until nobody could run any more.

They ate the sandwiches back in the warmth of the car, sand between their toes and all over the seats, trainers with socks stuffed inside lying abandoned on the floor. This side of the dunes, away from the chill of the screaming wind, the still air seemed warm and almost balmy. Soon they lapsed into a state of near-exhaustion, still hungry from all the exertion, so when Dad suggested going home for an early fish-and-chip dinner and a DVD, everyone agreed.

They were driving back towards the town of Whitehaven, Louis having claimed the front seat thanks to his map-reading skills, when a thought, or rather a feeling, occurred to him.

'Damn, I really need to piss.'

'Louis, your language, *please*,' Dad said.

Max groaned. 'You should have gone in the sand dunes like the rest of us!'

'What if someone had seen you?' Louis always got stage fright if he tried to go in public.

'There wasn't anyone *there*!'

'I suppose pulling over on this deserted stretch of road is out of the question,' Dad said.

'You supposed right,' Louis tersely retorted.

'I really don't know where we're going to find a public toilet around here,' Dad said. 'Perhaps when we get to Whitehaven . . .'

But in Whitehaven, everything looked closed and there wasn't a McDonald's in sight. 'I could try and sneak you into a pub . . .' Dad suggested dubiously.

'Oh, for goodness' sake,' Max huffed in the back seat. 'Can't you hold it till we get home?'

'No way,' Louis said, scanning the quiet streets. Suddenly his eyes happened on a sign for a railway station. 'Drive to the station – there'll be toilets there!'

In the deserted station car park, Louis took his feet off the sandy dashboard and hastily shoved them into his trainers.

Inside Whitehaven station, he took the steps two at a

time, and to his great relief found the men's toilets at the end of the windy platform. Pausing at the basins to wash the salt and sand from his face, he shook himself dry and emerged back onto the platform just as a train was pulling out. A thin stream of people were disappearing up the platform steps ahead and Louis followed them. When he reached the top, he paused to let an old woman past, and his eyes met a missing person's poster taped to the station wall.

Chapter Six

Later, he remembered very little of the journey home. After he'd stood, frozen, in front of the poster for what felt like an eternity, a small voice at the back of his head told him he needed to move before the others came looking for him. So he forced his legs, his stiff, shaky legs, to walk out of the station and across the car park and back into the car, where Millie was curled up on the back seat with her fingers in her mouth, and Max was complaining about how long he'd been, and Dad was starting the engine, eager to get home.

Sometime later, Dad glanced over at him and said, 'Are you all right?'

'Yes,' said Louis, feeling his throat constrict as he forced a smile.

'You're looking very pale,' Dad said. 'You were in

there for ages. Have you got an upset stomach?'

'No,' Louis said, and then, realizing that this could be a useful cover-up, 'I mean yes.'

Dad shot him another puzzled look, but fortunately the motorway seemed to be taking up the lion's share of his attention.

Every muscle in Louis' body was clenched tight but his insides felt as if they were shaking. He fixed a spot on the windscreen and concentrated hard on keeping his breathing even. He shut his eyes to deter any further questioning from Dad but, confined to the darkness of his own mind, his thoughts started to scream. What, oh what was going on? Had he imagined that poster? Was he losing his mind? No, the photos were clearly imprinted on his brain. That photo of Millie had been taken last month on the veranda, when she was twirling about, trying to copy Louis' triple spin. The photo of Max had been taken by Dad only a few months earlier, during their Easter trip to EuroDisney. The photo of himself was the one from the living-room mantelpiece, the one that Maman used to say made him look like an angel. Louis' eyes snapped open. What had Dad done? What had Dad *done*?

They stopped off at the fish-and-chip shop and Dad and Max went inside to order; Millie was fast asleep in the back. As they drove the last stretch home, the smell of the food turned Louis' stomach: he felt his mouth fill with saliva and it was an effort not to gag. When they pulled up in front of the house, Millie woke up and declared she was starving. There was still sand all over the floor of the car, and as they walked across the courtyard to the front door, Dad and Max wrestled with each other to see who could get in first.

In the kitchen, Millie rushed about with plates and ketchup, Dad went to empty their sandy shoes out of the back door, and Max tried to engage Louis in a discussion over which film they should watch. In the living room they sat around the coffee table with their plates and drinks, Max putting on the DVD and Millie arguing that Max had more chips than she did. Then Dad came in with his plate, sat down on the couch next to Louis and reached out and ruffled Louis' hair. 'The perfect end to the perfect day,' he said with a smile. And that's when Louis dropped his entire meal on the living-room floor.

All of a sudden, the room seemed drained of oxygen, and Dad, Max and Millie appeared to be nothing more than characters in a television programme. Louis had the terrible feeling that none of this was really happening, it was all an illusion, and really he was somewhere else – back at home in Paris perhaps – while someone was playing with his mind. He wanted to shout to himself, *Wake up! Wake up!* and find himself blinking at the dark ceiling, his heart still thudding, wondering why he'd had such a vivid dream. But instead of that, Max was swearing at him; Dad was saying, 'It doesn't matter, you can share mine,' scooping handfuls of soggy fish and chips up off the carpet, until Millie's voice, shrill with alarm, cut through the rest of the noise: 'Louis, what's the matter?'

He put his hands over his mouth to try and muffle the gasping sound that was escaping him, and Dad looked up and dropped the handful of food and grabbed him by the wrists and said, 'Louis, what's wrong? What's wrong? Are you hurt?'

At the touch of Dad's hands, an electric current shot through him and he jumped up, breaking free from his father's grasp and crashing backwards into the TV, shouting, 'Don't touch me! Don't touch me! You lied to us! Don't come near me! Maman has no idea where we are!'

Dad's expression suddenly crumbled and the colour drained from his face. His mouth hung open and he sank heavily back down onto the couch. Max froze, staring at them both, one hand still on the light switch. And Millie looked from one face to the other, finally running over to Max with a whimper and clutching his arm.

'Louis, how did you find out . . . ? I never meant for you to – I was going to tell you, I promise, I just needed some more time to plan exactly how . . .' Dad's voice was shaking, his eyes fixed on Louis'.

Max was breathing heavily, his eyes wild. 'Would somebody please tell me what the hell's going on?'

'Louis, please,' Dad tried. 'Let's just sit down and talk about it. I'll explain everything. I never wanted to lie to you—'

'Why?' Louis shouted at the top of his voice. '*Why?*'

Millie gave another strangled whimper, hands pressed over her mouth.

'Because I love you,' Dad said. 'Because I can't live without my children—'

'You had no right!' Louis yelled, feeling tears spring to his eyes. 'You had no right just to take us, without telling us, as if we were nothing but pieces of furniture—!' A sob escaped him and he slapped the back of his fist to his mouth, biting his knuckles.

'If someone doesn't tell me what's going on, *right now* . . .' Max warned.

Dad said, his voice still shaking, 'I can explain *everything*—'

'He kidnapped us!' Louis shouted, whirling round to Max. 'This whole holiday thing is a sham! The trip to Amsterdam was just to cover his tracks! Maman hasn't let us stay an extra week! Maman doesn't even know where we are!'

'Louis, please listen . . .' Dad tried again.

A look of horror was slowly spreading across Max's face. 'What do you mean, *kidnapped*?' he said slowly. 'You mean like a custody-battle thing?' He stared at Louis. 'How do you know?'

'Because I've just seen photos of us plastered on a missing person's poster in Whitehaven station!' Louis yelled.

'Oh God . . .' Dad's face was ashen.

'You're joking,' Max gasped.

'But how can he have kidnapped us?' Millie cried. 'He's our daddy!'

Louis turned to Millie. 'Maman doesn't know where we are! Nobody in France knows where we've gone! Dad took us away to live with him even though Maman won the court case!'

'Maman won the court case?' Millie burst into tears. 'But I don't want to just see Daddy once a month!'

'We won't have to!' Louis shouted. 'He's kidnapped

us! He's kidnapped us so that we have to live with *him* full-time and not with Maman!'

Millie sniffed, clearly still struggling to make sense of the situation. 'You mean we're staying here for ever? You mean we're never going back to Paris again?'

'Yes!' shouted Louis.

'No!' shouted Dad.

'Oh, this is unreal,' Max breathed, his voice weak with disbelief.

'What do you mean, *no*?' Louis demanded. 'Are you saying you'll let us go back to Paris right now?'

Dad put his head in his hands and fingered his thinning hair. 'Of course,' he said quietly. 'If that's what you want.'

'You're lying!' Louis shouted savagely.

'I wanted to give you the choice,' Dad said quietly. 'The court ruling in Maman's favour didn't give you a choice. This way I've given you a choice. Don't you see? Of course you can go back if you want. I'd never keep you *anywhere* against your will.'

'What, we can go back right now?' Louis shouted.

'Yes, right now,' Dad said.

'You wouldn't stop us?' Louis demanded furiously.

'Of course not. I would never force you to do *anything* you didn't want to do.'

'You're not honestly saying you did this just for *us*?' Max turned to Dad angrily. 'Just to give *us* a choice?'

'No,' Dad said. 'No. I was selfish. I was very selfish. I did this for me because I knew that I couldn't live without you.'

There was a long silence.

'If they've put our photos on a missing person's poster,' Max said slowly, 'does that mean you're wanted by the police?'

Dad nodded slowly. 'It would seem that way,' he said. 'But Whitehaven . . . Why – how would they know . . . ?'

'So if we choose to go back to France, you'd go to prison?' Max demanded to know.

Millie began to cry again.

'No, no, no,' Dad said quickly.

'Don't mess with us any more,' Max said quietly. 'Just tell us the truth.'

'Look,' Dad said. 'If you want to go back to Paris, I can just put you all on a plane. I don't need to fly back with you. And so nothing would happen to me.'

'But then we'd never be able to see you again,' Max stated matter-of-factly.

'That's not true. I'd just have to lie low for a while . . .'

'Just be honest for once, Dad,' Louis said acidly. 'If we choose to go back to Paris, you could face arrest! And one thing's for sure – you'd never have access to us again. So, by saying you wanted to give us a choice, you're actually forcing us to choose. Between living with you and never seeing Maman again, or living with Maman and never seeing you again.'

Dad rubbed his eyes with a soft moan. 'What else could I do? I lost the court case. My lawyer told me I had no chance with the appeal. It was either lose you completely, or give you this choice.'

They talked well into the night, the food congealing uneaten on their plates, Millie falling asleep on the floor with her head on Dad's lap. Finally, even Louis was sitting down, his back against the wall, knees drawn up to his chest, too tired to stand up and shout any more. Dad explained it all from the very beginning: when he first heard he had lost the court case he had just wanted to die. Then, one sleepless night, he had come up with a plan. Initially he had thought of taking them back to Ireland, but then he realized that Ireland was the first place the police would start to look. So he had contacted his old university friend Meg, in London, and asked her if she could help him. She had said yes, and with her help he had started getting the paperwork underway. But then, last month, Maman had told him that he could see the children for one last weekend. From then on, the visits were going to be supervised in the court's family centre. And so he had realized he was going to have to act immediately. Several weeks of frantic planning ensued, giving notice at the flat in Rueil and shipping belongings over to Meg's house in London. Meg helped Dad obtain false ID. She also said they could rent her holiday farmhouse in the Lake District for as long as they needed. And so here they were.

'And when were you planning on telling us all this?' Max asked him.

'I was going to tell you last Saturday, the night before you were due to go home. I was going to tell you everything, like I've done now, and give you the choice of staying with me here in England or returning to Paris. But then, at breakfast, Millie started asking if she could spend another week. And you did too, Max. And I chickened out. I thought, *If I stall for another week, maybe there's more chance they'll want to stay with me*. I never, ever reckoned on one of you seeing your face on a missing person's poster. Oh, God . . .'

Louis glared at him. 'Well, you reckoned wrong.'

'So that's why you took away my mobile phone,' Max gasped. 'And why you got Meg to cut our hair . . .'

'And why you wouldn't let Millie phone Mum to tell her about her new room,' Louis added.

'Yes,' Dad said. 'It was wrong. And horribly unfair on all three of you. But what else could I possibly have done?'

'You could have told us about the plan,' Louis said. 'You could have given us the choice of being involved, right from the beginning, instead of just snatching us like objects.'

'I thought about that, but the risk would have been too great,' Dad replied. 'You could have so easily let it slip, and even if you hadn't, it would have been hard for all three of you to put on an act in front of Maman.'

Louis thought about it and realized Dad was right. It would have been so easy to give the game away. Even if he had told them in the airport, someone might have overheard. 'So what happens now?' he asked.

'Now?' Dad spread his hands. 'Now it's completely and entirely up to you.'

Silence fell. Max bit his lip. 'That's not fair,' he said softly.

'It's not,' Dad agreed, putting his head in his hands. 'And I'm sorry. I'm so terribly sorry.'

When they finally went to bed, a pale dawn was beginning to leak through the curtains. Dad carried

Millie up to her room and Louis fell face down on his bed, not even bothering to take off his shoes.

When he awoke, the room was flooded with sunlight. The belt of his jeans cut into his side and his T-shirt stuck damply to his skin. He sat up groggily, the open curtains revealing a painful blue sky. Max was sitting cross-legged on his neatly made bed, playing a game on the laptop, his cropped brown hair wet from the shower. He glanced over at Louis. 'Morning, dozey.'

Louis sat on the edge of his bed, rubbing his eyes and running his fingers through his hair. 'What time is it?' he mumbled.

'Quarter past twelve. You were sleeping like the dead. Dad said not to wake you.'

'Has everyone had breakfast?'

'Ages ago. Dad's taken Millie out to lunch. He's going to try and explain things properly to her and ask her what she wants to do.'

Louis sat up, suddenly fully awake. 'You mean she gets to choose too?'

'Of course,' Max replied. 'What did you think?'

'I thought . . .' Louis hesitated. He didn't really know what he'd thought. That they were all going to make a decision as a family perhaps? 'What if Millie decides she wants to go back and we decide we want to stay here?' he queried. 'How is Dad going to make Millie promise never to tell anyone back in France where we are? She's crap at keeping secrets.'

'Dad said if any of us choose to go back, he'll move,' Max said. 'Like that there won't be any secret to keep. Nobody will actually know where he's gone.'

Louis pressed his fists against his closed eyelids, struggling to make sense of it all. His brain seemed to be enveloped by a thick fog this morning, and Max's chirpy demeanour on the other side of the room wasn't helping. 'So you mean, if Millie decides to go back to Paris and we decide to stay here, then we'll have to disappear with Dad again and never see Millie or Maman?'

'Only till we're sixteen,' Max said lightly. 'Then we can do what we want.'

'All right for you,' Louis said grumpily. 'That's only a year and a half away.'

'Four years isn't that long either,' Max added.

'Yes it *is* bloody long!' Louis suddenly shouted. 'If I don't see Millie for four years, she'll be nearly a teenager before I see her again! And if I don't see Maman for four years – do you have any idea how worried she'll be?'

'Relax, Louis,' Max said infuriatingly. 'She knows we're with Dad. He left her a letter. So she knows we're perfectly safe. She even knows we're in England – that's why you came across the missing person's poster. Dad just can't figure out why there'd be a poster in the Lake District . . .'

Louis' mind suddenly flashed back to the phone call to Pierre. *Papa took us on holiday. We're in a place called the Lake District.* He felt his heart skip a beat. 'Don't you think Mum has a right to know where we are?'

'No. Why should she? She was the one who was trying to stop us from seeing Dad, remember? Anyway, she's so busy with her clients and that new idiot she's dating, she probably won't even notice we've gone.'

Louis glared at him. 'Oh, this is just because you hate Charlot, isn't it?'

Max shrugged. 'It's only a matter of time before that schmuck moves in and starts forcing us to call him *Papa.*'

Louis went back to rubbing his eyes again and Max turned to the computer. Suddenly, Louis dropped his hands and stared across at his brother.

'What?' Max said uncomfortably.

'You've chosen, haven't you?' Louis said.

'So what if I have?'

'You're staying here with Dad, aren't you?'

'Why shouldn't I?' Max replied defensively. 'This place is heaps better than Paris. And if it means never having to go back to the Lycée . . .' He gave a little laugh. 'My God, it's a dream come true!'

'Don't you think Dad's going to make you go to school here in September?'

'Yeah, but over here they have A levels instead of the Baccalauréat – just two or three subjects instead of ten! And Dad's already said I can do my GCSEs by distance learning if I prefer.'

'Oh, great,' Louis said acidly. 'So you're basing your decision uniquely on the education system.'

'No. It's also because I want to live with Dad. He looked after us when we were little. He was always the one there for us. I'll miss Mum, sure, but she's never really around, is she? And when she is, all she does is criticize. Anyway, I'll be able to see her again in a year or so.'

'And Millie? What about if Millie goes back? What about if I go back?'

'Millie won't go back,' Max said. 'You know how crazy she is about Dad.'

'Ha!' Louis shouted. 'That's where you're wrong! Millie will go back! You've forgotten about Trésor!'

But when Millie came back with Dad after lunch, her face was pink and puffy and she went straight up to her room and closed the door. Dad sat at the kitchen table, his face grey. 'I never meant to put her through that, I never meant to put her through that,' he said.

Louis felt like shouting, *Well then, you should have thought about that before kidnapping us!* but didn't. Dad was clearly going through hell. He couldn't handle Louis' rage too.

In the afternoon, Max and Dad went out into the garden to erect a fence and Louis found himself tiptoe-ing up to Millie's room. He listened outside her door. Silence. He lifted his hand and knocked. There was a muffled sound from within. Louis turned the handle and went in.

She was sitting on her bed, wisps of her unfamiliar short hair sticking to her pink cheeks, her face still wet with tears, clutching her doll to her chest. Louis closed the door, then sat down beside her and put his arm around her as she snuggled up against him.

'Did Dad tell you?'

She nodded silently.

'It was a horrible thing to do. But I think he did it because he loves us,' Louis found himself saying.

'I know that,' Millie said. 'I just wish he'd taken Trésor too!'

Louis started in surprise. 'Is that why you're crying?'

'He was my favourite cat in the whole world!' A loud sob escaped her.

'What about Maman?' Louis asked.

'She doesn't like him! She'll probably give him away!' Millie sobbed.

'No, I mean what about not seeing Maman again? And all your friends at school? You won't see them again either.'

'I don't care about them! I just care about Trésor!'

'OK, but listen.' Louis decided to try another tactic. 'If you wanted to, you could go back to Maman and Trésor and all your friends in Paris. You don't have to stay here. You could go back with me.'

'But I don't want to go back!' Millie wailed. 'I want to live here with Daddy!'

'OK, Millie, listen.' Louis tried to disentangle himself from the wailing wet ball and look into his sister's eyes. 'You have to choose. You have to choose between Trésor and Daddy.'

Millie stopped crying suddenly and sniffed hard. She looked at Louis. 'Daddy said he would buy me a new kitten.'

Louis lay prone on the living-room couch, propped up on his elbows, staring down at the cushions. So that was it, he thought. He couldn't believe it. Millie was going to be bought off with a cat, and Max was going to be bought off with the promise of not having to go to school. OK, so perhaps that wasn't entirely fair. Both Max and Millie were closer to Dad than to Maman. Damn it, they all were! But that didn't mean he wanted to live on the run, in a strange country, speaking a strange language, going to a school where he knew nobody and would most likely be bottom of the class! He'd had a life in Paris! His best friend, Pierre, whom he'd known since he was four. His other friends, Luc and Henri, whom he'd known since primary school. His class at the Lycée, and of course his dance classes, where his teacher was giving him extra one-to-one lessons for free, and taking him to competitions up and down the country. How could Dad ask him to give all that up? How could he? But of course, he wasn't. *It's entirely up to you*, Dad had said. But now, if Louis decided he *did* want to go back, he'd be breaking rank, forcing them all to move house again just when they'd got this place halfway decent. And not only would he be losing his father, he'd be losing his brother and sister as well. Dad said he'd wanted to give them a choice. But what kind of choice did Louis have now?

Chapter Seven

They sat around the kitchen table staring at each other in silence. Dad had a small pile of papers in front of him. He leafed through them nervously.

'We're from a small village called Yaté, in New Caledonia,' he began. 'You went to the Lycée Malvin in Yaté. It was a small school, only a hundred pupils, and you were in the same classes as you were in Paris. Try not to give any more details than that. Yaté is that tiny place we stayed at during our holiday two years ago. I'm banking on the fact that we won't be meeting anyone from New Caledonia here in the Lake District. If by any chance you do, give them a wide berth.'

They nodded tensely.

'Your mother and my wife, Brigitte Franklin, died six years ago, when Millie was just two. She died of breast

128

cancer. If anyone asks you for more details than that, I want you to say you'd rather not talk about it.'

More nods.

'We came to England because I wasn't happy with the education system in New Caledonia,' Dad went on. 'I wanted you to be brought up in the British education system and eventually go on to British universities, like I did.' There was a pause. 'The first thing we need to do is give you new names,' he told them. 'Because I'm Jonathan Franklin, you'll all have to be Franklin too, but you can choose your first names.'

'How did you get false ID?' Max asked.

'Meg started by searching birth records for a child who was born in approximately the same year as me but who had died,' Dad said. 'She then applied for a copy of the birth certificate. When I arrived in London I was able to use the birth certificate to apply for other forms of identification such as a driving licence and national insurance number.'

'But what about us?' Louis asked. 'We can't just pinch the birth certificate of some random dead baby. We need to have the same surname as you.'

'Meg has a friend who is able to provide false documents,' Dad replied. 'When you've chosen your names, he will make up birth certificates and school reports for you.'

Louis, Max and Millie looked at each other. 'We get to choose our own names?' Millie piped up.

'Within reason,' Dad added with a little smile. His eyes looked tired.

'Does it have to be an English name?' Max asked.

Dad nodded. 'I think English or Irish would be best.'

'What about Hunter?' Max suggested.

Dad managed a chuckle. 'Keep thinking.'

'I want to be called Katie,' Millie said.

'Spelled how?'

'K – a – t – i – e.'

'Katie Franklin. OK, that works,' Dad said. 'Louis?'

'Lewis,' he said.

'That's Louis in English.'

'I know. I don't want to change my name.'

Max shot him a look.

'OK, fine. I don't know – Liam, then. That's English, isn't it?'

'Liam Franklin. OK . . . Max?'

'Joshua,' Max said with a grin. 'But you can call me Josh.'

Dad wrote out their new names on a piece of paper, along with a summary of their past. He left them to learn it off by heart while he drove into town to email Meg their new names so that she could supply them with the relevant documents. A strange sense of unreality settled over them as they lay around the room, trying to memorize the details of their new identity.

After a few minutes Max gave a laugh. 'This is so cool,' he said. 'It's like something out of *Alias*.'

'It isn't a game.' Millie glared at him. 'If we make a mistake, Dad could go to prison!'

'Sorry, Katie,' Max said, biting back a smile.

But Millie was also trying not to smile. 'That's all right, Josh,' she said.

Louis said nothing, and read through the details of his new life for a fourth time. I used to be called Louis Whittaker, he thought to himself. I had a sister called Millie and a brother called Max. I used to live in a big house in Paris. I used to go to a school called Le Lycée Maraux and I was top of my class in most subjects. My best friend was Pierre Duchard. I used to help him in class. I used to go to his house to eat chocolate biscuits and play on his computer. I used to do three dance classes a week and compete in competitions all over the country. I used to speak French every day. Now I don't know who I am any more. I have a name that means nothing to me – Liam Franklin. I have short hair. I'm only allowed to speak in English. I live with my father, Jonathan, my sister, Katie, and my brother, Josh. I no longer live in a big city in France but among hills and lakes outside a tiny village in England. And my mother is dead.

After dinner that evening, Dad kept them at the kitchen table. 'Right,' he said. 'I want to do a final run-through. This has got to be watertight, do you understand? Watertight. All it takes is one slip-up and people will start asking questions. In a small place like this, news travels fast.'

They nodded. Dad's face had a tense, hard look Louis couldn't remember seeing before.

Dad looked at Millie. 'What's your name?' He asked her.

'Katie,' she answered promptly.

'What's your surname?'

'Franklin.'

'Spell that.'

'F – r – a – n – k – l – i – n.'

'Where are you from?'

'New Caledonia.'

'Where in New Caledonia?'

'Yaté.'

'Where's that?'

'It's about, um – eighty kilometres south of the capital,' Millie faltered fractionally.

'And what's the capital?'

'Nouméa.'

'Nou*me*a,' Dad repeated, changing the pronunciation. 'Say it again in an English way. Nou*me*a.'

'Nou*me*a,' Millie said, her eyes wide and unblinking.

Dad turned to Max. 'Where's your mother?' he demanded.

'She died,' Max replied.

'When? How?'

'She died six years ago of breast cancer.'

'And your dad?'

'He's an accountant,' Max said smoothly. 'He moved us over here because he was fed up with the school system in New Caledonia.'

'What's your father's name?' Dad turned sharply to Louis.

'Jonathan Franklin,' Louis replied.

'What are your brother and sister called?'

'Katie and Josh.'

'Where did you used to go to school?'

'At the Lycée Malvin in Yaté.'

Dad sat back and exhaled slowly. 'OK,' he breathed. 'OK, OK, OK.'

'Dad,' Millie said softly. 'If we get caught, would you go to prison?'

Dad seemed to hesitate. Then he said, 'It's a possibility. But we won't get caught. We'll just be very, very careful.'

Louis couldn't sleep. The sense of unreality had still not lifted from his shoulders. Ever since he came across the poster with their faces in the train station, he had felt as if he was walking through some kind of dream – he kept expecting Dad to turn round and say, 'April Fool! Ha ha, I really had you there, didn't I?' Ever since the evening he had found out Max and Millie were going to stay with Dad in the Lake District, the evening he had told Dad that he too wanted to stay here, he had kept expecting Dad to change his mind, to suddenly call off the whole crazy plan . . . But despite his exhausted, caffeine-jittery look, Dad seemed to know exactly what he was doing. He was having some help, though, that much was clear. Every night, after they were in bed, he sat in the kitchen with the door firmly closed, on the phone to Meg. Louis heard him every time he got up to go to the bathroom, Dad's murmuring voice carrying on well into the night.

When would Pierre and Luc realize he wasn't ever coming back? Louis wondered. Would his form teacher have told the class that the Whittaker children had disappeared? Would Maman have been in to talk to the headmaster? Would his teacher have already struck his name off the register? His mind buzzed with possibilities and it was impossible to lie still. From his bed on the other side of the room, Max groaned. 'Louis, cut it out, will you?'

In a bid to get rid of his French accent, Max had started adopting an American one, aping the endless Hollywood films he watched. Louis thought it sounded daft, but Max seemed to be well into this reinventing-himself game, even persuading Dad to let him have his ear pierced. Louis thought back to the poster in the station and realized that Max no longer looked anything like the French teenager in the photo. He had a crew cut, his once-blond hair was a mousy brown, and he had brown contacts in his eyes and a gold stud in his ear – Maman would've had a fit if she could see him, and the Lycée Maraux would probably expel him on the spot. Millie looked pretty different too – her curly blonde bob made her look older and she had almost completely stopped sucking her fingers. She was beginning to sound more English too. As for Louis – well, thanks to Meg he no longer had a shaggy-dog hairstyle and the summer sun had browned his skin and brought out a smattering of freckles across the bridge of his nose . . . But he was still Louis Whittaker, Parisian schoolboy and red-hot dancer – wasn't he? Suddenly the urge to talk to someone from back home overwhelmed him. Did Pierre even remember him? Or had he already replaced him with a new best friend? Who did Luc walk to dance class with now? Wouldn't he be glad that Louis was out of the picture if it meant that he was the best boy dancer? The thoughts flickered across his mind like TV static until he finally fell into a splintered sleep.

On Thursday morning they drove into Kendal and went shopping again. First, they went to Marks and Spencer's and Dad made them buy socks and underwear. Then they went to Waterstone's and chose two books each. After that they went to WHSmith, where they bought a *Formula One* magazine for Max and felt-tips and a drawing pad for Millie. Finally, Dad offered to buy them a new outfit each. Millie dragged Dad to look at some summer dresses and Louis and Max departed for Gap to look at the jeans.

'Don't forget who you are,' Dad muttered before they went their separate ways. 'You're Josh and Liam now. And remember to speak English.'

In Gap, Max pondered over whether to buy 'loose fit'

or 'baggy' while Louis held up a pair of 'straights' against himself to check the length. When they had chosen their jeans, Louis found himself a grey T-shirt and blue hooded top while Max tried on the baseball caps by the till.

'That one doesn't suit you,' Louis said to him, forgetting to speak in English.

Max tried on another. 'What about this one?'

'Better.'

'This is so cool,' Max said. 'It's like we're aliens from Mars or something, and we have to buy everything from scratch.'

The sales assistant smiled at them as they came up to the counter to pay. 'Are you boys French?' she asked them.

There was a moment of flustered silence. Max and Louis looked at each other. 'No, we're from New Caledonia,' Max said quickly.

The woman raised her eyebrows. 'Where's that then?'

Max glanced at Louis.

'South Pacific,' Louis said.

'Crikey. You boys here on holiday, are you?'

Another hesitation. 'Yes,' Louis said. 'I-I mean no. We live here now.'

It was with some relief that they escaped from the shop.

'You've got to stop speaking French!' Max hissed to Louis as soon as they were outside.

'You were too!'

'But you started!'

After meeting up with Millie and Dad, they dumped their bulging carrier bags in the boot of the Peugeot and went to have lunch in a pub. Then Dad surprised them all by saying, 'I've got a job interview this afternoon.'

They all turned to look at him.

'It's in Windermere. It'll probably take a couple of hours, so I was thinking of leaving you at the cinema.'

'You're going to get a new job over here?' Max asked him.

'I have to, Max. We need the money.'

'Are you going back to working in a bank?' Louis asked.

'No, I couldn't get a job like that without references,' Dad replied. 'This is just for a small company owned by a friend of Meg's. They need a computer technician.'

'Are you going to be working all day, every day?' Millie asked.

'Depends if I get the job or not. But they operate flexitime and I won't be doing long hours, I promise.'

But when they got to the cinema in Windermere, they

found there were only three films showing, all ones they had already seen in Paris.

'This place is rubbish,' Max complained. 'It doesn't even have a decent cinema.'

'Well, you probably watch enough films as it is,' Dad said. 'Now, let me think ... I saw a sign for a leisure centre in town – let's see if we can find it and you can go for a swim.'

'I don't want to go bloody swimming,' Max complained.

'We don't have swimsuits, Dad,' Millie reminded him.

Dad sighed, looking tired suddenly. 'Let's just go and see, shall we?'

The leisure centre was in the centre of town – a very modern, glass-fronted building surrounded by a large car park. From the outside, they could see two floors of gym equipment – rows and rows of treadmills and exercise bikes and rowing machines and sweaty, lycra-clad men and women pumping their way to fitness. In the reception area they were hit by the smell of chlorine, and behind the desk, another glass wall overlooked a large, echoing pool, filled with noisy kids. Leaflets promoting karate, t'ai chi, yoga and pilates adorned the two large notice boards, and straight away Max saw something that caught his eye: 'Table tennis!'

Dad looked instantly relieved. 'That's for a club, but maybe we can just hire the bats and the table.'

Dad spoke to the receptionist, found that they could, and Max's mood instantly brightened. Dad paid for two hours and they were handed bats and balls and led down a long carpeted corridor to one of the indoor tennis courts where four table-tennis tables were set out, all empty. Max instantly set about trying to sell Millie the idea of being the ball girl, prompting a vigorous protest. Dad slapped Louis on the back and said, 'I'll be back at six o'clock at the latest, OK?' He gave them ten pounds for snacks and drinks and then left as Millie and Max continued their squabbling.

Five minutes later, and Max had got his way – he and Louis were warming up with a friendly rally while Millie stomped around, picking up balls. Then they started a best of three and Max's eyes narrowed in concentration. Soon they were playing hard. Max took the first set comfortably; Louis took the second by just two points. Max won the third, but only by a narrow margin. Louis was pleased: Max had always thrashed him in the past.

'My turn!' Millie begged as they collapsed on the bench. 'Please!'

'OK, OK.' Max stood up wearily.

'I'm going to get a drink,' Louis said.

'Get me a Coke,' Max said.

'Get me a Coke too,' added Millie.

Louis walked back down the wide corridor that over-looked the courts, brushing the damp hair back from his forehead. He wandered around the centre for a few min-utes, searching for the cafeteria, which he eventually found, and bought three cans of Coke. He opened one and began to drink thirstily. Then he paused as some-thing caught his eye. A flyer on a notice board:

COME DANCE!
WINDERMERE JUNIOR DANCE CLUB –
STREET, MODERN, BALLET AND JAZZ,
EVERY MONDAY AND THURSDAY AT 5 P.M.
IN THE DANCE STUDIO.

A dance club? Louis checked his watch. It was ten to five. Still sipping from his Coke can, he found another corridor and wandered down it, passing changing rooms and shrieks from the pool. He passed the double doors to the gym, heard music and followed the sound down to the end of the corridor, but it only led to a large room full of spandex-clothed women doing aerobics. Perhaps this was what they called the dance studio. Oh well. He left the stamping women and began to head back to the tennis courts.

'Have you come for the class?'

A voice from behind made him start. He swung round. A girl of about his own age had come out of the door at the far end of the corridor, beyond the aerobics class, and was looking at him enquiringly with large green cat's eyes. She wore a scrunchie round her wrist and her long dark hair hung loose around her shoulders – damp and tangled, almost reaching her waist. She was startlingly pretty, her pale skin contrasting sharply with her hair, freckles covering her cheekbones, her mouth wearing the hint of a smile.

'No. I was just looking for the – um – dance studio,' he said, flustered.

'It's here,' the girl said, pointing behind her.

'Oh.' He noticed now that she was wearing a black leotard under her red tracksuit bottoms and moved with the grace of an experienced dancer.

'Have you come for the class then?' the girl asked, looking him up and down.

'Well, no,' Louis said awkwardly, feeling himself blush. 'I was just – um – looking around. I wanted to see what it looked like.'

'Just looks like an ordinary dance studio,' the girl said,

turning back towards the open door. Louis followed her.
'It's big though.'

It was huge. Polished wooden floors and floor-to-ceiling windows. A dozen teenagers sat on the floor at the far end, chatting and changing their shoes.

'Are you a dancer?' The girl was scrutinizing him again.

'Well, not really. Kind of. I used to do a bit, back where I came from.'

'What kind of dance?'

'Street-dance, tap and – um – ballet.'

The girl looked impressed. 'Were you any good?'

He shrugged, embarrassed.

'Can you do a triple turn?' she asked him.

'Yeah.'

'Quad?'

'Yeah.'

'Jeez. What else can you do?'

'Tumbling and stuff.'

'Backflips?'

'Yeah.'

She looked at him in disbelief. 'Show me?'

'Not here!'

'Do you want to join our class? It's advanced jazz. Miss Kano, our teacher, would be thrilled. We've only got two boys in the class and she's always trying to recruit more.'

'I can't . . .' Louis stepped back. 'My brother and sister are waiting for me. We're playing table tennis.'

The girl gave a small shrug. 'OK, well, see you around.'

'Yeah, sure,' Louis said. He held out one of the unopened cans. 'D'you want a drink?'

The girl smiled and took it from him. 'Thanks,' she said, then turned round and went back into the studio.

'What the hell took you so long?' Max was hitting balls against the raised side of the table and Millie was sitting on the floor trying to juggle.

'Here,' Louis said, handing Millie a Coke.

'What about me?' Max sounded outraged.

'You'll have to share – they only had one left,' Louis said.

Max muttered angrily to himself and grabbed the can from Millie as she struggled to open it. 'You were ages! Did you get lost or something?'

'Yes,' Louis replied.

That evening, after dinner, Max threw himself down in front of the TV and Millie brought her dolls' house down to the living room to play with. Louis was on his way upstairs to read his book when Dad emerged from the kitchen, his hands still foamy from the washing up. 'I need to go to the village shop to get some more milk for breakfast,' he said.

Louis stopped, one hand on the splintered banister. 'D'you want me to go?'

'Why don't you come with me?' Dad suggested.

'There's no point in us both going,' Louis snapped.

Dad cocked his head. 'Come on.'

'Why?'

'Come on,' Dad said again, and went back into the kitchen to dry his hands.

They walked down the stony track in the golden evening light. The sound of crickets filled the air. It was a good fifteen-minute walk into the village, but for some reason Dad wouldn't take the car. There was a warm breeze that smelled of summer, but in his T-shirt and jeans, Louis shivered.

'You cold?' Dad asked.

'No.'

A silence. They walked side by side but with a space the size of another person between them.

'Louis,' Dad said after a while.

'What?'

'I know you're upset.'

'I'm not upset.'

Dad sighed. 'Well, you're not very happy then, that's for sure.'

Another silence.

'I want you to be happy. You, Max and Millie. That's all I care about.'

'No,' Louis said. 'You care about *you*. You care about *your* happiness.'

'That's true, I want to be happy too.' Dad sighed. 'But not at your expense. The most important thing is for my children to be happy.'

'And so that's why you took us away?'

'I took you away because I wanted to give you the chance to live with me. But also because I believed that, ultimately, you would be happier with me than with your mum.'

Louis said nothing.

'But maybe I was wrong,' Dad said. 'Do you think I should send you all back?'

Louis looked up at him sharply. 'The others want to stay with you.'

'I could tell them I'd changed my mind. That I realized I couldn't manage on my own.'

'Then we wouldn't be able to see you again.'

'Only for a little while,' Dad said. 'Until all the fuss had died down.'

Louis shrugged. 'No. The others want to live with you. I suppose I do too, really.'

'Then why are you so miserable, my love?'

Louis took a slow breath. *Because I had a mother*, he wanted to say. *She wasn't always a good mother. She worked long hours and snapped at us a lot and was always rude about our father. But she was our mother.* But he couldn't say it.

'Why do you and Mum hate each other?' he asked instead.

Dad sighed. 'Louis, we don't hate each other, we just stopped loving each other. It happens sometimes. People change. They grow apart.'

'I don't believe you,' Louis said. 'You do hate her. Otherwise why would you have taken us away from her?'

Dad said nothing for a moment. He seemed to be choosing his words carefully. 'Hate is a very strong word,' he said at length. 'When a marriage breaks down, it ends a lot of hopes, a lot of promises, a lot of dreams. It's hard not to feel angry. And it's hard not to feel bitter. And with all that anger, all that bitterness, it makes it very hard for those two people to put their heads together and agree on what's best for the children.'

'But why did Maman want us to stop spending weekends with you?'

'Because she was angry. Because she was upset.

Because she tried to convince herself I was an unfit father. She's a strong woman, your mum. She doesn't tolerate weakness.'

'She thought your nervous breakdown was a sign of weakness?'

Dad sighed. 'People started taking sides. Friends of ours saw me falling apart and tried to help, and she saw that as a betrayal of sorts. She got very angry. And anger can cloud judgement; it can make even good people do some very, very bad things.'

'Like you?' Louis said quietly. 'Like you taking us?'

Dad paled suddenly. And said nothing.

Chapter Eight

Dad got the job and started work on Monday. He had managed to arrange it so he would only go into the office in the mornings, then work from home in the afternoons. That way, he reckoned, he would be back not too long after they got up. On Monday morning, however, Louis woke at the sound of Dad's alarm. He found himself listening out for the sounds of his father getting ready – the shower, the radio, the kettle, the toaster, and eventually the click of the front door and the sound of the car starting up outside. Louis got up to pee and, from the bathroom window, watched the blue Peugeot bumping its way slowly along the dirt track under a hazy morning sky. Then the car turned and shot off down the main road, disappearing from sight.

Millie was up too, still in her nightdress, stirring

chocolate powder into a bowl of milk and cereal at the kitchen table, creating some kind of revolting paste. 'What are we going to do while Dad's at work?' she asked him.

'I dunno.' Louis shrugged, putting on some toast. 'Ask Max.'

'Ask Max what?' came a voice behind them, and Max entered wearing only his jogging bottoms, stretching and yawning loudly.

'Ew,' Millie complained. 'You're getting hairy armpits.'

'Shut up,' Max said lightly. 'It's going to be a scorching day today. I heard it on the weather forecast.'

'I'm going to wear my new summer dress!' Millie announced happily.

Max helped himself to the toast from the toaster. 'That's mine,' Louis protested.

Max sent the smaller of the two pieces spinning across the table. 'Stop being such a baby.'

Spreading butter on his remaining piece of toast, Louis said, 'We could go swimming.'

'What? I'm not going all the way to Windermere leisure centre.'

'I meant swimming in one of the lakes,' Louis said.

Millie's eyes widened.

Max looked at Louis suspiciously. 'Which lake?'

'Any lake,' Louis said. 'There are loads of them.'

'I want to swim in the lake!' Millie announced.

'Shut up,' Max said. 'You'll drown.'

'I can swim!' Millie protested loudly. 'Louis, please can I come?'

'We can all go,' Louis said.

Max hesitated. 'We don't have any swimming trunks.'

'We can wear shorts.'

'What about me?' Millie demanded.

'You can swim in your knickers. There'll be nobody around.'

Max grinned. 'OK, let's do it!'

They packed their rucksacks with towels and a change of clothes, locked up the house and went over to the barn to fetch their bikes. Even though it was only ten o'clock, the sun was already high and bright in a cloudless sky. They set off slowly, Millie wobbling precariously on the uneven track. Louis led the way, and once they got out onto the road, they picked up speed, Millie crowing in delight. A warm breeze lifted Louis' hair as he stood up on his pedals, and for the first time since the seaside, a feeling of well-being rushed through his body. As the road began to steepen, his breathing quickened and the back of his T-shirt stuck damply to his skin. He glanced behind him to make sure that Max and Millie were still in sight and then pressed on. Finally, the road began to even out and they turned off onto a grassy track, freewheeling downhill. Beneath them, the lake stretched out like a giant pool of ink and the wind caught Louis' T-shirt, making it billow out behind him. He heard the crunch of stones beneath his wheels as he raced, flat out, down towards the water's edge.

He skidded to a dizzying halt amidst a shower of pebbles and dry earth and waited for the others to join him. They threw their bikes down in the long grass and advanced tentatively to the water's edge. Louis dipped in a sandaled toe. The water was very cold and very clear. He could see a shoal of tiny fish swimming just below the surface.

Millie squealed in delight. 'Eeek, it's freezing!'

Max kicked off his trainers and started unbuttoning his jeans, uncovering a pair of shiny blue football shorts. He took a run from the grassy edge, but stopped short when he reached knee-deep water. 'Aargh, it's really cold!' Arms held out for balance, he advanced slowly, making loud gasping noises.

Millie stripped down to her knickers and began wading in, shrieking softly. Louis pulled off his T-shirt and sandals, following them in.

Millie was giving them a running commentary of

what she could feel underfoot. 'Ow, ow, it's sharp! Yuck, yuck, it's slimy!'

For a while all three of them advanced slowly, arms outstretched. Then suddenly Louis stumbled on a stone and the water rushed up to his waist. He yelped and then dived in. The cold water hit him like a slap in the face and for a few seconds all he could do was kick and swim and swim and kick and surface for a deep breath and then swim some more till finally the shock wore off enough for him to be able to turn round and look back at the others and shout breathlessly, 'Come on, it's great!'

Max and Millie shot him looks of disbelief as he continued to gasp with shock. He turned and swam out further, his arms and legs still lashing out against the cold, his muscles shuddering in protest. As he reached a spot about a hundred metres from the shore, he stopped and took a deep breath and sank down under the water, pushing himself as far down as he could go. His feet did not meet solid ground. The lake seemed bottomless.

When he re-emerged, heaving, he saw the others were finally in – Millie swimming a fast breaststroke and emitting a series of shrill yelps. Max swam over to Millie and started to splash her and the yelps turned into screams. Louis did a fast crawl to join in, and soon the water began to lose its icy grip and they could breathe without shuddering. The sun shone at full wattage from a brilliant blue sky and the air was heavy with the scents of summer. On the other side of the lake, a group of hikers, complete with boots and sticks, moved slowly up one of the hills. In the distance, beyond the cluster of stone houses in the village, the brown track snaked its way gently up the hill towards the farmhouse. Their farmhouse. Their home.

Louis tipped over onto his back, watched his toes appear, felt his ears fill with water, and gazed up at the dazzlingly bright sky. Millie let out a shriek. 'Louis! Louis, help! Max is drowning me!' Louis ignored her cries and continued to float. Unlike in the sea, there were no waves. The water was still, flat, glassy. The sensation of tranquillity was overwhelming. After a while he tipped back upright again and found he had drifted out to the centre of the lake. All around him, the dales towered up towards the sky. Golden sequins dappled the water. The shore was nothing more than a faint grey line in the distance. Squinting against the glare of the sun, Louis could just make out Millie, climbing the bank towards the footpath where they had left their bicycles, in search of a towel. Louis skimmed his hand against the water's surface and sent up a fine shower of droplets over his head. They caught the colours of the rainbow as they fell.

Something closed around his ankle and he was suddenly yanked downwards, deep into the water. Bubbles flew out of his nose as he writhed and kicked, fighting for the surface. Arms flailing, he managed a frantic gasp and Max laughed in his face before dunking him under again. This time he swallowed a mouthful of water and emerged gagging for breath. 'Max, you're so dead!' Louis managed to grab hold of Max by the shoulders and, using his full weight, rammed his brother down under the water. Max headbutted him in the chest and resurfaced, grabbing him by the leg. Louis freed himself with a kick.

'Race you to the shore,' Max shouted.

Louis sighed and tried to look reluctant. Then suddenly, he threw himself into a fast crawl.

With a yelp of protest, Max followed, churning up the water behind him. Louis speeded up, desperate to lose him. He'd had a headstart but it wasn't much and Max was a fast swimmer. And the patch of green was further away that it had appeared. Max was gaining; once or twice Louis felt the brush of Max's hand against his leg. Louis tried to break away.

When Louis' foot finally met muddy, stony ground, he was gasping. Max splashed through the water behind him, yelping. Suddenly, he threw himself forward and grabbed Louis' leg, trying to pull him back into the water. Choking with laughter, Louis attempted to wade up the muddy bank, Max a ball and chain round his ankle. 'I won, I won!' he yelled.

'No, you've got to touch the grass!' Max yelled back.

Louis belly-flopped into the shallow water, reaching out towards the grassy bank, trying to kick his leg free. But Max hung on grimly and for several moments they both just thrashed around, neither of them going anywhere.

'Cheater, cheater!' Louis was yelping.

Max hooked his arm around Louis' neck, forcing him down into the water. Louis felt his brother's knee against his back, and when he resurfaced, spluttering in rage, he saw that Max had climbed over him and was dragging himself up onto the grass.

'You lousy cheat!' Louis shouted, and half gasping, half laughing, splashed out of the water, wincing as the soles of his feet met the sharp edges of small stones, scrambling up towards Millie, who sat shivering beneath three layers of towels. Max and Louis grabbed their towels off her and began rubbing themselves down, springing from foot to foot against the chill of the gentle breeze, now an icy wind against their wet, goosefleshed skin. Louis pulled on his damp T-shirt, his denim shorts clinging wetly to his thighs, and towelled his hair vigorously until it fell back into its usual tousled mop. Max was attempting to wring out the water from the bottom of his shorts and Millie was still sitting there, shivering. Louis picked up her dress and put it over her head.

'No!' she protested. 'I don't want it to get wet!'

'It's going to get wet anyway,' Louis replied. 'Put it on – you'll be warmer.'

Grumbling, she obliged, threading her arms beneath the pink straps. Louis picked up her towel, rolled it up and put it back in her rucksack.

Max suggested food and so they cycled back towards the village, Max trying to scare Millie by shooting down past her without touching his brakes, Millie's shrieks echoing against the hillside. They left their bikes in the main street and stepped into the oily fug of the burger bar. The burly man at the counter recognized them and asked them where their dad was and Max told him about the job interview in Windermere. Then they ordered and sat around a grubby formica table. As they began to tuck in, a noisy group of school kids entered, jostling and shouting and laughing and chatting. Millie looked up in surprise, hurrying to finish her mouthful so she could speak. 'Why are they all dressed the same?'

'It's called school uniform,' Max told her. 'It's what they wear to school in England.'

'They have to wear ties to school?' Her eyes widened in disbelief. 'Will we have to go to school here in England?'

'We will in September,' Louis told her. 'After the summer holidays.'

'So you'll have to wear a tie then,' Millie informed him.

'You will too,' Louis said.

'Girls don't wear ties, silly.'

'Yes they do,' Louis replied, turning round in his seat. 'Look at that girl' – he pointed to a long-haired brunette who was waiting for her order – 'she's got—' He broke off as the girl, holding her tray of food, turned round. There was a surprised silence.

'Oh, hello,' said the girl.

'Hello,' Louis said, his mouth suddenly dry.

Another silence. The girl turned away again to say something to her friend.

'Who the hell is that?' Max hissed.

'How come you know her?' Millie asked, her voice very loud.

'She's just a girl I bumped into the other day at the leisure centre,' Louis whispered back angrily, flushing at their conspicuous reaction.

'What?' Max sounded outraged. 'When?'

'What's her name?' Millie wanted to know.

Louis gave Millie a vicious kick under the table as the girl suddenly moved away from her friends and came towards their table. 'Hi,' she said again. 'Are you brothers and sisters?'

'Yes,' Louis said quickly, pressing his foot hard against Millie's. 'That's my brother – um – Josh, and my sister, Katie.'

Millie clapped her hands over her mouth to stifle a giggle. Max elbowed her, hard, and she stopped.

'I'm Tess,' the girl said. 'What's your name?' She was looking at Louis.

'Liam,' Louis said, his cheeks hot.

Millie took a deep breath and held it. Max glared at her.

'Are you new around here?' Tess asked.

'Yeah,' Louis said.

'We come from New Caledonia,' Millie said in a rush. 'But we live here now.'

Max shot Millie a warning look.

'New Caledonia?' Tess repeated. 'Is that a country?'

'It's an island in the South Pacific,' Louis answered quickly.

'Wow.' Tess looked impressed. 'And so now you're living here in Grasmere?'

'No,' Millie said. 'We live in the old farmhouse above the village.'

'Oh, I thought that was the Daniels' holiday home.'

'It used to be,' Max said quickly. 'But we're renting it.'

'Oh.' She eyed them all with interest. 'So, are you all dancers?'

Millie burst into giggles again.

'No way,' Max said with a dramatic roll of the eyes. 'Just him.'

Louis shot Max a look of fury.

'Louis is really good,' Millie pitched in. 'He can do *grand-jetés* and *fouettés* and backflips and one-handed cartwheels . . .'

Tess was frowning. 'I thought you said your name was Liam,' she said to Louis.

There was an awful silence.

'That's – er – Louis is just his nickname,' Max stumbled, a flush spreading across his cheeks.

'Yeah,' Louis pitched in desperately. 'My name's Liam. Katie just calls me Louis and Loulou and stuff like that for fun.'

'Oh, right.' Tess gave an easy laugh. 'Well, it was really nice to meet you all. Liam, you should really consider coming to the dance classes at the Windermere leisure centre. They're every Monday and Thursday at five.'

* * *

That evening, at dinner, they told Dad about their morning spent at the lake. Dad expressed immediate concern about them swimming out of their depth and so Max quickly lied and assured him they hadn't. They then told him about the girl in the burger bar, leaving out the bit about Millie's slip-up. Dad looked really pleased. His eyes brightened still further when Louis mentioned the dance class. 'That's a great idea,' he said. 'Thursday at five? We can all drive over and I'll give Max a game of table tennis.'

'And me, and me!' Millie piped up.

'Of course "and you", sweetheart. Do we need to get you any special clothes, Louis?'

'Pink tights and ballet shoes!' Max choked on his own wit.

'Tracksuit bottoms and jazz shoes,' Louis replied, shooting Max a withering look.

'OK, I'll have a look in the phone directory and see what I can find,' Dad replied.

In the bed on the other side of the room, Max was sprawled on his back, one arm above his head, breathing deeply. A thin shaft of clear moonlight slanted between their beds and across the floor. Louis lifted up his arm to look at his watch. The luminous dial read a quarter to one. He couldn't sleep. He wished he could fast-forward to Thursday. He wished he could fall asleep. But sleep was one of those strange things which only crept up on you when you weren't thinking about it. He wondered what the dance class would be like. Maybe he'd be the only boy. Maybe he'd be so stiff from all this time off that Tess would think he had been boasting. He pointed his toe beneath the covers. Turned his leg out and raised it gently up from the mattress. Then, with a flick, he bent his knee and extended his leg towards the ceiling, sending the duvet slithering down to the floor.

He got out of bed and padded from the room. He crossed the landing: snores were already reverberating from hehind Dad's closed door. He crept down the stairs, unlocked the front door and walked out barefoot into the night.

The tops of the dales were hidden in mist and a strong full moon hung low in the night sky. The air was very still, very quiet, as if the entire world was holding its breath. The farmhouse, the car, the barn all looked unfamiliar in the strange white light. The cold, sharp stones of the courtyard were suddenly replaced by soft grass as Louis walked down to the bottom of the garden, gazing out towards the hills.

He stopped, placing his feet in fourth position, and did the slow arm movements of a *port de bras* to silent music, the soles of his feet stroking the damp grass, a gentle breeze tickling his bare skin. In the moonlight, his T-shirt and pants were a ghostly white and his arms almost silver. He took his hands up above his head, breathing in deeply, lifting his leg to *arabesque*, pulling in his stomach, raising his chin and staring out at the line that separated the earth from the sky. Slowly, very slowly, he tilted his weight forward and lifted his heel off the ground.

'Wow!' The word was only whispered, like a tiny puff of air, but it gave Louis such a fright that he toppled forward and swung round with a terrified gasp. A small figure had appeared at the edge of the grass and was crouching down, her pink nightdress pulled tight over her knees.

'Millie, it's the middle of the night! Go back to bed!' Louis whispered loudly.

'*You're* not in bed,' she replied.

'Dad will have a fit!'

'I can't get back to sleep.' She looked at him, the whites of her eyes bright in the moonlight. 'Do that again.'

He hesitated, then, realizing Millie wasn't about to go

back inside, lifted up into *arabesque* again, working hard at getting the line just right.

'Beautiful,' Millie murmured.

He brought his extended leg round to the side, then pulled his foot in sharply, turning a double *pirouette* to finish. Millie gasped in delight.

He did another *port de bras*, then brought his leg up into *attitude*, turning slowly on his supporting leg. 'Why can't you sleep?' he asked Millie.

She looked up at him. Her bob was growing out, her curls almost reaching her shoulders, and her face looked angelic in the moonlight. 'I had a dream,' she whispered.

'What dream?' he asked her, taking a deep breath and arching his back to bring his foot and head closer together.

'A dream about Maman.'

Louis stopped, frozen in *attitude*, then slowly lowered his leg back to the ground. 'A bad dream?'

'I dreamed we were back living with her again.'

Suddenly, Louis felt cold. He sat down on the grass, wrapping his arms around his knees. 'D'you miss her?'

Millie started to nod very slowly, and then her eyes were glistening.

'Millie . . .'

'D'you think she remembers us?' She pressed her

hand against her mouth and a muffled sob escaped her.

'Yes, of course she does!' Louis moved towards her on his knees and Millie instantly curled up against him.

'I want to see Maman again!' she sobbed quietly, her face wet against his T-shirt.

'We will,' Louis whispered. 'We will, Millie. One day.' And above him, the starlight blurred and fragmented into a kaleidoscope of unfallen tears.

Thursday. A fine drizzle fell over the dales so no one felt like swimming. Max spent the morning at the kitchen table, trying to fix a glitch in the laptop while Millie lay sprawled out on a rug, watching cartoons on TV. Restless, Louis pushed the sofa back and practised doing handsprings and backflips while Max complained about the table shaking.

When Dad came home from work, they had a late lunch, then drove to a sports shop in town to pick up a table-tennis bat for Max and some tracksuit bottoms for Louis; the shoes they had ordered online had still not arrived, so he would have to manage with the everyday ones he had. They arrived at the leisure centre early and so all four of them had a game. As the giant clock above the basketball net inched its way towards five, Louis began to feel nervous. He left the others to their game, dived into the toilets to change out of his jeans and then began the long walk down the corridor towards the dance studio. What if he was the only boy in the class? What if the class was already full? What if the teacher refused point blank to let him join in without proper shoes?

The dance studio was already busy. Louis stepped through the open door and hovered on the threshold. Two girls were practising *pirouettes* by the barre. Four other girls sat on the floor by the wall, chatting and changing their shoes. A black boy and a red-head were practising spinning on their head, break-dance style. A woman with cornrows, wearing a leotard and tracksuit bottoms, got up off the floor and came over. 'Can I help you?' she asked.

'Yes, um – I've come for the jazz class.'

At that moment a voice behind him said, 'Oh, excellent, you decided to come after all! Miss Kano, this is Liam, the boy I was telling you about.'

'Oh!' Miss Kano's face broke into a slow smile and she held out her hand to Louis. 'Nice to meet you. Tess seems to have taken it upon herself to recruit boys to join this class. You've had some dance training before, I gather?'

'Yeah, mainly street, ballet and tap.'

'Oh, wonderful, wonderful. Well, by all means join in and see how you get on. Have you got shoes?'

Louis explained about the delayed mail order.

'OK, well, fold your socks down below your heel so that you don't slip. Tess, are you going to lead the warm-up for me?'

'Give me some decent music then,' Tess said. She flashed Louis a grin and he smiled back shyly. She was wearing a blue leotard today and baggy black jogging bottoms. Her hair was still loose and unkempt, giving her a slightly wild look.

After a standard ten-minute warm-up to the beat of Lemar, led by Tess, Miss Kano took over. Louis kept to the back of the room, carefully watching the others in the huge mirror. The class was much smaller than the one he'd belonged to back in Paris, but the standard was high. Tess was by far the best – at once graceful and powerful, with beautifully elegant lines, technically fault-less. He could see that Miss Kano valued her too – whenever they came to a particularly difficult move, she got Tess to demonstrate. Several of the other girls were very 'ballet', with turned-out feet and graceful arms. The short red-headed boy was like a powerball, whereas the black guy was tall and skinny and obviously a Michael Jackson fan. After practising turns from the corner and step leaps across the room, the class picked up a routine they had been learning and Miss Kano told Louis to take a break. He sat down on the floor at the front of the room against the mirrors, swigging from his water bottle and watching the dance carefully. When he'd seen it performed a couple of times, he got back to his feet and joined in.

At the end of the class, Miss Kano beckoned him over to the front where she was kneeling, sorting through a collection of CDs. As the others jostled noisily for the door, Louis approached and sat down opposite the teacher, brushing the damp hair back from his forehead.

'How did you find it?' Miss Kano asked him.

Louis smiled and nodded. 'Great.'

'Think you'll come again?'

'Yep.'

'You're very good,' Miss Kano said with a little smile. 'I bet your old teacher was sorry to lose you.'

Louis thought of Madame Dubois and the Rouen competition they had been working so hard for. He said nothing.

'See, I told you!' Tess crowed, sliding over on her knees. 'He's even better than Jimmy! A real-life Billy Elliot!'

Miss Kano laughed. 'I think I agree!'

Louis said nothing, embarrassed suddenly. *Billy Elliot* was his favourite film in the world. He had begged Dad to take him to London to see the musical.

'He's the perfect partner for me!'

'Hold on,' Miss Kano said with a smile. 'I haven't even told him about the competition yet.'

'So? I'm telling him now.' Tess leaned forward on her hands, her green eyes shimmering with gold. Her face was so close, Louis could almost count the freckles sprinkled across the bridge of her nose. 'How old are you?'

'Twelve and a half.'

'You're tall for your age. I'm fourteen. But look, we're the same height. Will you be my dance partner in the Junior Pair Dance Competition? Please?' she asked. 'I've been looking forward to it all year, but last month my partner Jimmy suddenly announced he was giving up dancing to concentrate on fencing.' She snorted in disgust.

Louis stared back at her, momentarily mesmerized by those cat's eyes. 'OK,' he said.

Chapter Nine

By mid-July, life had slid into some kind of routine. They had been in England for nearly a month now and were officially on their summer break. The village centre was crowded with holiday-makers in waterproofs and walking boots, and the dales and lakes were speckled with hikers and bird-watchers. Early each morning, while Louis, Max and Millie were still in bed, Dad left the house and went to work. The children surfaced later, took their time over breakfast and then, if it wasn't raining, cycled over to one of the lakes for a swim. Afterwards they cycled home, bums soaked and hair dripping, stopping at the village for Cokes and magazines, returning home to read (Louis), draw (Millie) or play computer games (Max) until Dad arrived with food. After a late lunch they would drive out somewhere – either to the beach or to a neighbouring town, or to an amusement park. Evenings were spent watching films while Dad worked at the kitchen table. Initially, Mondays and Thursdays were dance nights for Louis and table-tennis nights for the rest of the family. Then Dad found a tennis club for Max in Windermere, and a judo class for Millie at the local school, so Louis started cycling to his classes.

His dancing began to improve. Miss Kano was an exacting teacher, regularly keeping him and Tess behind after the rest of the class to work on a particular turn or difficult step sequence. By the time Louis emerged from the emptying leisure centre, he was sweaty and exhausted. He walked round to the car park with Tess, where her mum – a very large woman with a sixties-style hairdo and a cigarette permanently wedged between her lips – sat in her beat-up Fiat, its engine idling. Every time, she offered Louis a lift, and every time Louis declined, pointing towards his bike chained to the railings. Tess would say bye, giving Louis a quick kiss that always made his cheek feel even hotter, then slam into the passenger seat and start arguing with her mum before they had even pulled out of the car park. Finally, Louis would cycle the five miles home and arrive, cheeks blazing and calves throbbing, to wolf down a huge dinner and throw himself half dressed into bed, completely knackered.

Millie made a friend at judo called Natasha, who lived in the village, and promptly invited her over to spend the night. Dad was worried at first – worried that there would be a slip-up with the new names, but after a million assurances from Millie, he relented, and a small red-head with pointy features turned up one evening and spent the entire time holed up with Millie in her bedroom. A week later, after a game of tennis, Max turned up unexpectedly with a spotty-faced beanpole called Ned – Max introduced Louis as 'my little brother, the ballerina' and the two of them hogged the computer and the living room all evening.

The following night, at dinner, Dad said to Louis, 'I think it's your turn to invite someone over.'

Louis shot him a look. 'My friends all live in France.'

Dad fell silent for a moment. Then he said, 'What about that girl you dance with – Tess, isn't it? The one with *the most amazing feet*?'

Max and Millie burst into laughter. Louis said nothing. (It had been an on-going joke ever since he'd come back from his first dance class in Windermere, and had made the mistake of telling the others that Tess had the most amazing feet. Feet? Max had guffawed. *Feet?* Even Millie had laughed.)

'But she's a girl, Daddy,' Millie pointed out.

'So?' Dad replied. 'I don't remember there being any law against girls and boys being friends!'

Millie giggled.

'The girl in the burger bar?' Max said. 'Yeah, invite her over. She seemed cool.'

'Yeah, yeah. Maybe,' Louis replied.

He had no intention of inviting Tess over to the house for Millie to giggle at and Max to make boy-ballerina jokes to. Besides, Tess was two whole years older than him and didn't see him as a friend – just as a freakishly good dancer, as she kept on saying: 'But how did you get so good? I mean, I've done ballet and jazz since I was about three. My mum had some wild idea that I was gonna be a child star or something – look how that turned out.' Laughter. 'But you're a boy. Boys don't usually dance like you do.'

'I had a friend in primary school,' Louis replied, remembering Luc. 'We used to try and outdo each other in the playground, body-popping and break-dancing. Then he started doing all these great new moves and I found out he'd started street-dance. I started to pester my parents and eventually they gave in.'

'Don't you miss your friends and stuff?' They were sitting on the wall that flanked the now empty car park after their Monday dance class, waiting for Tess's ride. 'New Caledonia's the other side of the world. I don't suppose you can go back very regularly.'

Louis scuffed the heel of his trainer against the wall and looked out across the car park. 'I won't be able to go back till I'm sixteen.'

'Why?' Surprise sounded in her voice.

'Because – because my father doesn't want me to, that's why. When I'm sixteen I'll be able to do what I like.'

'He couldn't stop you even now, surely,' Tess said. 'I mean, if you found a way to get the money—'

'He couldn't stop me, but he would be very upset,' Louis said carefully. 'He – he has bad memories of that place.'

'Why? Because it's where your mother died?'

'Yeah . . .'

'That must have been awful,' Tess said. 'I'm really sorry.'

Louis looked away from her, for fear that his face would betray his emotions. *No!* he wanted to shout. *No, she's not dead! No, she's alive and well and living in Paris! But she will be going out of her mind not knowing where we are. She will be furious with Dad. She will have contacted her lawyers and the police and our photos will have been plastered on posters all over the country.*

'What?' Tess said.

He turned back to her. 'Nothing.'

'You looked really angry for a moment.' Silence. 'There's Mum.' She jumped down from the wall. 'See you Thursday – don't forget to practise the axel turn!'

He waved her off and then unchained his bike and cycled home.

That evening, Max lay face down on the sofa, which had been relegated to the end of the room so that Louis could practise his dance moves while watching his reflection against the darkness of the living-room window. Dad was upstairs, reading Millie her bedtime story.

'Oh, for Christ's sake,' Max said as Louis' backflip caused the TV remote to fall off the edge of the couch.

Louis broke into some fast *fouettés*, counting aloud. Max took his eyes off the television screen for a moment.

'How many can you do in one go?'

Louis broke off, heaving for breath. 'Thirty-two.'

'Can you still do that one-handed cartwheel?'

Louis demonstrated.

'Cool.' There was a silence. Max turned his eyes back

to the television, but Louis could tell he wasn't really watching it. Louis stared hard at his reflection in the living-room window and performed a slow *développé*.

'D'you ever miss Paris?' Max asked him suddenly.

His leg extended in the air in front of him, Louis moved his arms slowly into fifth position. 'Yeah. All the time.'

'What d'you miss the most?' Max asked him, his eyes still on the television screen.

'Maman,' Louis said.

'I miss her too,' Max said. 'I mean, she used to drive me insane with her nagging and everything, but sometimes she was OK. I bet she's furious with Dad.'

On Thursday, Miss Kano beckoned them over and the three of them sat down cross-legged beside the stereo. 'The details of the Junior Pair Dance Competition have finally come through. The regional heats for our area are going to be held in Preston at the end of August. Semi-finals and finals are in London.'

Louis and Tess exchanged looks. Tess snatched the papers from Miss Kano's hand. 'Runner-up prizes are a thousand pounds. Grand prize is a performance in the Royal Variety Show!'

'What's the Royal Variety Show?' Louis asked.

Tess handed him the flyer. 'It's an annual show featuring the likes of Elton John and Graham Norton, with dance acts and music acts and stand-up comics. It's usually held in some grand venue like the London Coliseum and attended by major celebrities and even the Queen.'

Louis exhaled slowly.

'Well, let's keep our feet on the ground,' Miss Kano said. 'There are five age categories, and children from all over the country will be entering. But it would be a good experience for your first competition.'

Tess shot Louis a grin.

'What dance are we going to do?' he asked.

'We'll have to get to work,' Miss Kano replied. 'There's no time to spare. I'll need you both for a full hour after class every Monday and Thursday and we'll need to meet for two hours Saturday mornings as well. Say ten?'

They nodded.

'Fine then. I'll see if I can book the studio for Saturdays and I'll give you both a call to confirm. But between now and then I need you to dig out your three favourite pieces of dance music – suitable pieces, obviously. A medium to fast beat would be best. I'll see what I can come up with too and we'll pick the music and start the choreography on Saturday.'

'Have you ever entered a dance competition before?' Tess asked him as they sat waiting for her ride.

'Yes, a few. I was due to go to one just before we – just before we left.'

'I've only been in one before, and it was organized by the local drama school, so it didn't really count. I was only ten and I came second. I was so upset I cried.'

'Please don't cry if we don't win this one,' Louis said with a little smile.

Tess's eyes were bright. 'But imagine if we did win,' she said. 'The Royal Variety Show. We'd be on telly. Wow!'

Suddenly, the musical sound of a demented frog erupted from her pocket. She pulled out her phone, answered it, and a rapid volley of words burst out of the handset. 'Oh, not again,' Tess said. 'Yeah, OK . . .' She sighed. 'Yeah, OK . . . Yeah, OK. I'll walk . . . Yeah, OK. Bye.' She clicked the handset shut.

'That was my mum,' she told Louis. 'The stupid car's gone and broken down again. I'll have to walk home and it'll take me hours.'

Louis looked at her. 'D'you want a lift?'

She stared at him in surprise, then at the bike, still chained to the railings. 'How?'

Louis jumped down from the wall. 'See these two bits

here?' He said, pointing to the metal prongs on either side of the back wheel. 'You can stand on them and then hold onto my shoulders. My sister does it all the time.'

'Yeah, but I'm quite a bit bigger than your sister.'

'Let's try,' Louis said. 'It's practically all downhill anyway. I'll take you back to the farmhouse and then my dad can give you a lift down to the village.'

'OK.' Tess bit her upper lip and looked worried as Louis unchained his bike. Then, once he'd straddled it, she cautiously climbed up onto the metal prongs, tightly gripping his shoulders. Louis put his foot up on the pedal, bracing himself for the extra load. 'Ready?' he said.

'I think so.'

Standing up on the pedals, Louis pushed off. There was a wobbly moment when the wheel turned sharply sidewards and the bike nearly toppled over, but with a few grunts he managed to get the wheels properly in motion and once they picked up some speed, it was fine.

'Don't crash, Liam.'

'I'll try not to.'

'My life is quite literally in your hands.'

The sun was turning golden as they left the town behind them and they began to pick up speed on the long, winding descent, Tess's fingers tight against Louis' shoulders. The wind lashed at their faces and whipped tears from their eyes and Louis stood up on the pedals, freewheeling down the road, Tess letting out a small gasp whenever the tyres bumped against a crack or a stone. The wheels whirred softly against the smooth tarmac and sequinned sunlight fell through the branches of overhanging trees. The long empty road stretched ahead of them, snaking its way into the distance as far as the eye could see.

When they arrived at the farmhouse, after bumping their way along the seemingly endless dirt track, they found Millie out front, cradling something in her arms.

'I saw you coming up from the road. Look what Daddy bought me. Look, look!'

It was a kitten, a very small, jet-black kitten with a white stripe along its nose.

'Oh, cute!' Tess exclaimed. 'Can I hold her?'

'It's a *him*,' Millie announced proudly. 'And his name's Treasure.'

As Millie carefully transferred the kitten into Tess's arms, Louis shot her a look. 'You already have a cat called Treasure,' he reminded her coldly.

'No, I don't. Trésor is a French name and he's a French cat. And he's not mine any more.'

'I think that's a lovely name for a cat,' Tess said. 'It

suits him perfectly. Isn't he adorable, Liam? Look at that tiny pink nose . . .'

They had entered the hallway now, stumbling through the clutter of newspapers, trainers and plastic bags that littered the floor. The kitchen was warm and fuggy, the oven was humming, and Dad sat poring over his laptop. After being introduced to Tess, he immediately insisted that she stay for dinner and so she rang her mother while Louis set an extra place at the table. Dad gathered up his work stuff and put it away and asked Tess polite questions about her family, her school and the GCSE courses she was about to embark on. Apparently embarrassed by the lack of greenery on the evening menu, Dad threw together a hasty salad and Tess insisted on making a complicated-looking vinaigrette. Millie was oblivious to them all, with eyes only for her new kitten.

'Well, Tess, I hope you like lasagne,' Dad said as he lifted the heavy dish from the oven and began serving. 'After Liam's dance classes I know that only stodgy carbohydrates will do.'

'I love all food, especially Italian,' Tess replied with feeling. 'Smells great.'

'Right, well, I think we're just about ready,' Dad said as Louis filled the jug with water. 'Katie, will you go and call your brother please?'

Millie was crawling under the table after the kitten. 'Why can't Liam?'

'Katie, *now*,' Dad said, in a voice which clearly meant: *Don't make me lose my temper when we have a guest*. 'And take the cat out of the kitchen while we eat.'

'But he's new – he'll be frightened all alone—' Millie began to protest, breaking off as Dad fished her out from under the table and propelled her firmly towards the door. 'Go. Now.'

She went reluctantly, the kitten following her, and a moment later returned, minus the new pet, and plonked herself grumpily down at the far end of the table.

'Glasses, Katie,' Louis said to her.

'You're nearer the cupboard!'

'Glasses are your one and only job!' Louis retorted.

Tess got up quickly. 'I can do it—'

Louis glared at his sister. 'Katie!'

She jumped up, hurried over to the cupboard and began to set the glasses out with a lot of noise. Tess went over to help her. Dad finished dishing up and they all sat down. Then the kitchen door opened and Max's eyes widened with surprise.

'Hello,' he said.

Tess smiled. 'You remember me then?'

'Little Liam's dancing buddy.' Max grinned. 'Course I

do. How are you?' He sat down, pushing up his sleeves and revealing a pair of deeply tanned arms.

'Fine, thank you,' Tess said, her cheeks suddenly pink.

'Liam and Tess have been asked to perform in a dance competition together,' Dad told Max.

'Really?' Max raised his eyebrows. 'That sounds great.'

Louis sighed inwardly. Since when had Max been interested in his dancing?

'We're going to start choreographing it this Saturday,' Tess said. 'We've got to find some good music first.'

Dinner was a strange affair. Tess kept asking polite questions about their life in New Caledonia while Dad kept trying to change the subject. Millie talked endlessly about the damn cat while Max cracked jokes which only Tess seemed to find funny.

'So what does Liam look like in tights?' he asked Tess at the height of his wit.

'Shut up!' Louis snapped.

'Actually, none of us wear tights,' Tess replied, biting back a smile. 'But Liam's really amazing. Miss Kano says his technique's brilliant and he's got star quality. She thinks he should audition for the London production of *Billy Elliot*.'

Louis stared down at his plate and felt his cheeks flush.

'Ooh, Liam is blushing!' Millie crowed.

'Katie . . .' Dad warned.

'Of course, I'm pretty good too,' Tess said, and they all laughed.

After dinner, Louis managed to persuade Max to lend them his iPod and he and Tess went into the living room to hook it up to the television speakers.

'How come you haven't got a stereo or any CDs?' Tess asked.

'Um – well, we've only been here a month and we left most of our stuff behind in New Caledonia.'

'Really? Why?'

'Because – um – it was too heavy to transport. We figured it would be easier just to replace stuff when we arrived.'

Tess looked unconvinced, but didn't force the issue. After several minutes of fiddling, Louis finally got the speakers to work.

They trawled through Max's endless hip-hop collection, interspersed with the odd Ashanti/Robbie Williams/Lemar track. Now and again either Louis or Tess would get up off the floor and perform a few moves to the music to check the beat. But most of the time they just listened, facing each other on the patterned carpet with pen and paper handy to jot down any ideas. Tess sat with her back against the couch, knees drawn up, wisps of brown hair falling into her face. Louis sat cross-legged, chewing on his thumbnail, trying to picture the dance moves in his head. When they got to Bomfunk MC's *Freestyler*, Tess suddenly sat up and said, 'This could work.'

'Too fast,' Louis replied.

'Yes, but all the other dances are going to be medium-beat, Lemar-style,' Tess countered. 'This would be the perfect tempo for stuff like spins and tumbling – your speciality.' She stood up and kicked off her shoes. 'Come on, let's try some stuff.'

'What, now?' Louis asked, embarrassed.

'Yes! We don't have to do any tumbling – we can just mark it.' She pushed the couch against the wall and started to move the coffee table. Hesitantly, Louis got to his feet and began to help her. Within seconds they had a decent space. Tess went over to the iPod, put the track back to the beginning and turned the speakers up loud.

'Starting positions,' she declared, and struck a comical pose, laughing.

Louis began to smile. 'Something simple,' he said. 'Simple starting positions are always the best.'

'Back to back?' Tess suggested.

They tried it. 'We're almost exactly the same height, so that might work,' Tess said, turning her head.

'What are you talking about? I'm definitely taller!' Louis countered jokingly, rising onto his toes.

Tess laughed and nudged him with her bum, sending him toppling forward. She put the track back to the beginning again. 'Legs together or apart?' she asked.

'Apart,' Louis said. 'Else we'll look like telegraph poles.'

'Arms only to start?'

Louis tried a few things.

'You look like a windmill,' Tess said.

Louis exaggerated the windmill effect and they both laughed.

Tess demo'd some arms. 'Like this?' she suggested. 'Or this, or this?'

'The first one,' Louis said. 'And then we could turn round and do some mirror-image stuff.'

'Half turn or proper turn or double turn or what?'

'Half turn just so we're facing each other,' Louis said. 'We'll save the spins for later. Start off really easy. So we face each other and do the same arms and then add a bit on, like this . . .'

'Oh, yes, I like that,' Tess agreed.

'Hey, hey, no – I know,' Louis said suddenly. 'We do

mirror-image when we're back to back and then non-mirror-image when we're facing each other—'

'Brilliant!'

Louis put the track back to the beginning. They took up their starting positions, back to back, then twisted their heads round to look at one another, and laughed.

'We can't do that,' Louis said.

'No. Just look straight ahead,' Tess agreed.

The music started. 'Five, six, seven, eight . . .'

Millie came in and stood in the doorway just as they began. 'Oh, please let me see the whole thing!' she said as they broke off.

'That's all we've got so far,' Louis told her.

'Is that the dance you're going to do in the competition? It's really good!' Millie enthused. She scooped up the kitten and sat with him on the relegated couch. 'Treasure and me will be your audience,' she said.

'No, come on, Katie, you're distracting us,' Louis said.

'Oh *please*!'

'She can stay, can't she?' Tess said to Louis. 'Maybe she can give us some ideas.'

Louis shot Millie a look but said nothing.

'From the top?' Tess suggested.

Louis nodded.

When they came to the new bit, Louis stopped,

chewing on his thumbnail, thinking hard. Tess tried out some fresh moves. Millie stood up and did a twirl, her pink dress spinning out around her. 'Why don't you do this?' she cried.

Tess laughed. 'Oh, look at her, Liam, she's so sweet! She could be our lucky mascot or something!'

Louis looked at his sister. And wondered why he suddenly hated her.

On Saturday morning, Miss Kano was suitably impressed. 'Wouldn't have been my first choice of music but I really like what you've done with it so far. I think we should keep going with this. You've got an excellent introduction – now we need to start building it up a little.'

'The cool stuff!' Tess rubbed her hands together with a gleam in her eyes. 'Spins and tumbling!'

For the next hour and a half they worked on the middle section of the dance, linking step sequences to some of the bigger elements. By the time they got round to having a break, the windows had steamed up and Louis' hair was plastered to the sides of his burning face. He glugged thirstily from his water bottle while Tess and Miss Kano discussed the subject of shoes – notably how to get around the problem of needing trainers for the tumbling and dance shoes for the step work.

'We can incorporate it into our dance!' Tess joked. 'The changing-shoes scene!'

Louis chuckled at the thought.

'Seriously,' Miss Kano said, 'we need to get it right or one of you could end up with a broken toe. Let's stay in trainers for the time being and I'll have a scoot around the net tomorrow and see what I can come up with.'

'She's pretty decent, Miss Kano,' Tess said as they sat on the wall in the heavy midday heat, waiting for Tess's ride. 'I've known her since I was six. She taught me ballet in the church hall. Then she started a modern-dance class, jazz and tap. She teaches them all herself.'

'Why isn't she a professional dancer?' Louis asked. 'She could be – she's that good.'

'She used to be,' Tess replied. 'She was in a couple of West End shows. But then she got married and moved up here. You've got to be in London to be a professional dancer.'

'Oh,' Louis said.

'She calls me her borrowed daughter,' Tess went on. 'When I was little, she used to take me down to London in the school holidays to see the Royal Ballet— Hey!' She broke off as Louis downed the remains of the Coke. 'Have you finished it all, you greedy pig?'

'It's so hot,' Louis said in his defence. 'I'm dehydrated.'

'Well, stop sweating all over me then,' Tess retorted, shaking imaginary droplets off her arm. 'God, it's scorching. You know what I'd really love to do right now? Dive into Easedale Tarn, or Rydal Water, or Grasmere—'

'Why don't we then?' Louis looked at her. 'Me and my brother and sister swim in Easedale Tarn all the time.'

'Now?' Tess said.

'Now,' Louis replied.

'But I don't have my swimsuit.'

Louis chewed his lower lip. 'Now that could be a problem.'

'Wait a minute,' she said. 'I'm so stupid! I've got my leotard on under my tracksuit. That'll do!'

As soon as Tess's mum arrived, she was sent off again, muttering about being nothing more than a taxi service. The cycle home with Tess on the back was tougher this time, under the beat of the midday sun. When they reached the farmhouse, Louis felt ready to pass out, red blotches pulsating in front of his eyes. Dad gave them the usual lecture about not going out of their depth as Millie tried to persuade Max to let her bring Treasure along. Louis went to find Tess a towel. Then they set off, Millie riding on Max's handlebars, Tess on the raised saddle of Millie's bike.

The water felt wonderful on Louis' sun-scorched skin. He sank beneath the surface and felt the itchy, salty sweat melt away into the breathtakingly cold, clear water. They had started swimming in another lake now – it was a bit further from the farmhouse but more secluded from the holiday hikers, shut-off by towering mountains on every side. There was even a waterfall cascading down the side of the mountain and into the far end of the lake about half a mile away. Millie was climbing up onto Max's shoulders and diving off. Tess was swimming a swift, elegant crawl, right out towards the island in the centre of the lake. Louis decided to follow her.

It was a long way out, further than he'd first realized. At one point he thought of heading back, his arms and legs still aching after all the dancing and cycling. But then he forced himself to press on. If Tess could do it, why couldn't he? About a hundred metres ahead of him, he saw with some relief that Tess was now wading through the water towards the grassy bank of the island. When he reached her, he was spent, his leg muscles trembling with exhaustion as he clambered over the sharp stones onto the muddy bank.

Tess was lying back, breathing hard. Louis threw himself face down a little further away and for a while neither of them said anything, struggling to catch their breath. Then he raised his head from his arms and looked at her through the tall grass. She was still lying down. He could make out the water droplets glistening on her cheek. Her chest rose and fell rapidly. She had her eyes closed. Louis rolled onto his side and propped his head up against his hand.

'Boo,' he said.

She didn't jump. Instead she opened one eye and turned her head, squinting against the glare of the sun. 'Is that you, Liam?'

'Yes,' Louis replied.

There was a silence. Tess closed her eyes again. Louis waited. She didn't move. Her breathing slowed. A drop of water ran down her cheek, pearling on her earlobe. 'Your name isn't really Liam, is it,' she said.

It wasn't phrased as a question. A pounding began in his chest. A rushing in his ears. After a very long silence he managed, 'What do you – what do you mean?'

She opened her eyes. Turned her head to look at him through the grass. 'Your name's Louis, isn't it?'

Breathing hard, Louis sat up cross-legged. 'I – I already told you. Liam is my name. Louis is my nickname.'

'I don't believe you,' Tess said evenly. 'No one has a completely separate name for a nickname. Louis is a French name, isn't it? And you *are* from French-speaking

New Caledonia – or did you lie about that too?'

Silence. Louis felt as if his insides were trembling.

'And I'll bet your brother's name isn't really Josh. And your sister's name isn't really Katie. Neither of those names are French as far as I know. And you *are* French, I know that much, because of your accents.'

'I'm *not* French – I mean, I *am* French,' Louis stumbled. 'I'm French-speaking, but I'm from New Caledonia.' His head was spinning and he suddenly felt violently sick. *Max, help!*

'Oh, I get it, you're not even from New Caledonia.' Tess sat up slowly, folding her long legs and resting her chin on her knees. 'This is getting more and more interesting. Where are you from then?'

Jesus, Louis thought desperately, *have I given the whole game away?*

Tess narrowed her eyes at him. 'Why are you looking so scared?'

Louis swallowed, not trusting himself to speak.

'I'm not trying to be horrid,' Tess said. 'I'm just curious. Why are you lying about your names and where you come from? Did your dad rob a bank or something? Are you in hiding?'

More silence.

Tess's expression sobered even further. 'Is it serious?'

Louis looked down at the ground. It was an effort to breathe.

'Louis . . .' Sitting up, concerned now, she touched his arm.

His head shot up. 'You mustn't tell anyone. You've got to absolutely promise not to tell anyone! Not Max, nor Dad, nor Millie. They'd go crazy if they thought you knew!'

'Of course, Louis, I promise,' Tess said. Her hand was still on his arm.

Louis leaned forward and put his head in his hands. 'Oh God, I can't believe it's coming out already. I can't believe we only managed to last barely over a month—'

'Hold on, hold on,' Tess said reasonably. 'Nobody else knows, I'm sure. If people thought you were hiding something, it would be all round the village, and nobody's said a word. It's only me who's guessed. And that's probably only because I've been spending so much time with you.'

Louis ran his hands through his wet hair, trying to resist the urge to pull it out. 'If you tell anyone . . .' he began. 'If you tell anyone, I mean *anyone*—'

'What, you'll come back and slit my throat?' She started to laugh, then quickly disguised it with a cough. 'No, seriously, I won't tell anyone, Louis.'

He took a deep breath, then exhaled and spoke very fast. 'You're right, my name *is* Louis. And Josh and Katie are really Max and Millie. We're from Paris. And our dad is wanted by the French police for something called non-custodial child abduction.'

Tess's eyes widened. 'Whoa. You mean your mum's *alive*? Your dad kidnapped you from your *mum*?' Her voice was incredulous.

'Yeah, exactly.'

'No way,' she breathed. 'How did he abduct you?'

'He didn't really. It's just the term they use. We thought he was taking us on holiday. When we found out what had happened, he gave us the choice of going back. But as it meant choosing between staying here with Dad or going back to Paris and never seeing him again, we chose to stay here.'

'But what about your mum?' Tess looked aghast. 'Don't you miss her?'

'Yes, of course, but she was never really around. She's a broker in a big trading firm – she's always worked long hours. When we were little, before we went to school, Dad was the one who gave up work and stayed home to look after us. It's not that we don't love our mother, we've just never been that close to her, that's all.'

'Christ!' Tess exhaled slowly. 'This is unbelievable!'

They fell silent for a few moments and Tess chewed on a long shoot of grass, elbows on knees, staring out across the lake. Louis followed her gaze and suddenly they were both aware of Max and Millie, tiny specks on the other side, jumping up and down, shouting and waving.

'Oh, no,' Louis said, scrambling to his feet. 'Millie's probably getting cold and wants to go home . . .'

They ran back into the water, gasping with the shock of the cold on their sun-dried skin. As they waded in, Louis suddenly stopped and grabbed Tess by the arm. 'You really do promise—?'

'I really do promise, Liam,' she said, switching back to his fake name. 'I like you, crazy dancer-boy. I'd never do anything to hurt you or your family.' And she leaned forward and kissed him on the cheek before turning and diving back into the water.

Chapter Ten

That night, Louis couldn't sleep. Long after Dad's bedroom door clicked shut, he found himself still staring at the ceiling, his heart pounding. *I could end this,* he thought, *right here, right now, with just one phone call. I could have the police here before morning, I could have Maman on the next plane out, I could be back at the Lycée, back in Paris, back with my friends in the blink of an eye. It is all so fragile, this new house, this new life. How easily I could crush it. And perhaps I have already taken the first step by telling Tess, by sharing our secret with someone from the outside world, someone I've only known a few weeks, someone I have no idea whether I can trust. So why did I do it? Because she guessed something was up, because she cornered me for answers – true, but that couldn't have been the only reason. After all, I could have told her another story, made up another excuse for having to cover our tracks. But I told her the truth and, with that one conversation, risked everything! Yet strangely, all I felt was relief – relief at having shared this secret, relief at having told Tess something real about me and, for a moment at least, relief at having been able to be myself again.*

But as the days went by, Tess appeared true to her word. She never showed the slightest flicker of amusement when using their names. She stopped asking any questions about their previous life. And she only ever brought up the abduction when she and Louis were alone. Which was less and less frequently. Of course, there were the dance classes, but Miss Kano was present then, and they were having to work very hard to get the dance routine sorted out in time for the competition. Now that school was out, Tess baby-sat three days a week, and at the weekends helped her mother in the stationery shop they owned in Windermere. On her days off, however, she usually cycled round to the farmhouse. She came swimming with them, she made pancakes with them, she played Barbies with Millie in her bedroom and basketball with Max in the courtyard. But most of the time she practised dance moves with Louis outside to the beat of hip-hop on the new stereo Dad had finally got round to buying.

Millie would appoint herself music-controller, for lack

of anything better to do, and sat next to the stereo on the sill of the open kitchen window overlooking the garden, one hand on the pause button, the other round her Barbie's hair. Louis and Tess shouted out 'Stop', 'Go' and 'From the top' at intervals, to which Millie responded eagerly, if not always very accurately. Now and again she hopped off the windowsill and down onto the grass, and suggested some dance moves of her own, which Louis would ignore and which Tess would make polite noises to. Max dribbled the ball up and down the courtyard and practised shooting into the basketball net Dad had erected above the door of the barn.

Above them, the sun beat down from a cloudless sky. It was hot, really hot, the kind of dry heat that you can feel actually roasting your skin. Louis had stripped down to his vest and already his hair was damp against his forehead and his tracksuit bottoms stuck to the backs of his knees. Tess was wearing cut-off jeans and an over-sized T-shirt that skimmed her thighs. They were practising the last part of their routine – now that the step sequences, spins and tumbling were out of the way, Miss Kano had asked them to come up with some good *pas de deux* moves.

'I know,' Tess was saying. 'We can do that classic ballet pirouette where you put your hands on my waist and I turn four times and end in *arabesque*.' She demonstrated.

'So what do I do?' Louis asked.

'You have the easy part. You just put your hands on either side of my waist. Not too tightly, though, because you've got to give me room to turn.'

They tried it. Halfway through the pirouette, Tess's knee hit Louis' leg. He stepped backwards, she lost her balance and they both ended up in a heap on the ground.

'You should end it like that,' Max said, bouncing the ball off Louis' head as he lay prone, Tess sprawled on top of him. 'That way you'll definitely stand out.'

Tess laughed, disentangling herself from Louis. 'Sorry, sorry, let's try again!'

They got to their feet and resumed their position. 'Five, six, seven, eight . . .'

OK until the third turn. Then Tess lost her balance again and fell against Louis' chest. He grabbed her and staggered backwards and she hung her arms round his neck.

'Hopeless!' Millie cried gleefully.

'Sorry, sorry!' Tess laughed into Louis' T-shirt, her arms still around him, panting. She felt warm and her breath tickled his cheek. Her arms were brown from the sun, brushed with fine golden hairs.

The third time they tried, they met with the same result. 'You're pulling me off-balance!' Tess complained.

Louis laughed and said something about her pirouettes making him dizzy. But for some reason he didn't want them to get this move right. He really didn't want the dance to end. It only took a small shift in balance for her to fall against him. He only had to pretend to get mixed up with a particular step sequence for her to instantly take his hand and, head lowered, staring at his feet, carefully map out the required movements with him. Dancing with Tess today was like having permanent butterflies in his stomach – he felt at once giddy, light-headed and extremely alive.

Eventually, too hot and tired to continue, they returned to the relative cool of the kitchen and Louis set about making iced smoothies while Tess splashed her face with water at the sink. Millie was trying to do *pirouettes* round the kitchen table and Louis snapped at her in French to stop it, causing Tess to look up at him in surprise.

'What?'

'I've never heard you speak French before. That's so cool. Sounds nothing like the French we learn at school.'

Louis shrugged, embarrassed, and Millie piped up, '*Moi, je parle français parfaitement!*'

Tess laughed in delight. 'What does that mean?'

'She said she speaks perfect French,' Louis translated, frowning at Millie in annoyance. 'She's showing off, as usual.'

'Oh, that's so cool!' Tess exclaimed. 'Liam, you say something.'

He took the ice cubes out of the freezer and poured out the drinks. 'What?' he asked, embarrassed.

'I don't know. Say something to me. Preferably something nice.'

Louis pulled a face, his mind suddenly a blank. '*T'es jolie*' – the words escaped him with a will of their own. 'I mean – *t'es gentille*.'

'What does that mean?'

'You're nice.'

'No it doesn't! No it doesn't!' Millie crowed. 'He said *t'es jolie*, which means *you're pretty*!'

'Shut up, Katie! I said *t'es gentille*!' Louis yelled, the blood hot in his face.

'Liar! You said—' But Tess cut her off, grabbing her by the hand and bending down to whisper something in her ear. Louis glared at them both suspiciously.

Millie's eyes widened and she began to grin, then she turned and whispered something in Tess's ear.

'Look, do you two want a drink or not?' Louis asked in annoyance.

Tess straightened up, grinning. She looked at him. '*T'es meenon,*' she said.

Louis stared at her. 'What?'

Tess looked at Millie for help.

'*T'es mignon!*' Millie crowed. 'You're cute: *t'es mignon, t'es mignon!*'

Tess tried again. '*T'es mignon.*'

Louis felt his cheeks burn; he picked up his drink and rolled his eyes to the ceiling. 'You two are loonies,' he said. But inside his chest, his heart was thumping as if ready to burst.

That night, Louis lay face down on his bed, wearing only his boxers. It was too hot for a T-shirt; it was too hot for any blankets. The window was wide open, revealing a large patch of night sky. Max was playing his GameBoy on his bed, still fully dressed. His bedside lamp cast a puddle of light on the floor. From the room next door, they could hear Dad's voice as he read Millie her bedtime story.

'So,' Max said suddenly, without looking up, 'do you fancy Tess or what?'

Louis stopped breathing.

Max still didn't look up, but wrestled with the buttons, the sound of electronic firing erupting from the machine.

'What are you talking about?' Louis managed.

Max shrugged and glanced up. 'Do you honestly think Tess fancies you? You clearly fancy her.'

Louis tried to steady his breathing. He gripped the edge of his pillow hard. 'No. I don't – I'm not—'

'Oh, come on,' Max said. 'You were all over each other today.'

'That's because we were dancing!' Louis protested. 'It's a pair dance. We *have* to touch each other. We have to—'

Max just chuckled infuriatingly.

'I don't fancy her,' Louis said.

'You *so* do.'

'I don't!' Louis exclaimed hotly. 'She's just my dance partner, that's all.'

'Really?'

'Yes!'

'You should be careful though,' Max said.

'What d'you mean?'

'She's going to start asking questions.'

Louis said nothing and closed his eyes, breathing heavily into his pillow.

But his conversation with Max played on his mind that night. Did he fancy Tess? No. Of course not. Why? Because she was a teenager and he didn't turn thirteen for another four months. He had never fancied a girl before. Even if he *did* fancy her, there was nothing he could do about it. He didn't know how to kiss a girl. In films it always looked so easy, but there must be some kind of technique, some set of rules. And how were you supposed to know whether to do it or not? How were you supposed to know whether she wanted to? You couldn't very well ask. But when he closed his eyes, he could see her face so clearly: that dark-brown hair, those big green eyes, the sprinkling of freckles across her cheeks. He found himself imagining what it would be like to actually kiss her. Deep down he knew he really wanted to, even though it scared him.

'D'you want to go for a cycle ride?' It was Tess on the phone. She had called their new landline while they were in the middle of lunch and had asked to speak to him.

As soon as Dad had said her name, Louis had felt his heart begin to pound. Now he was gripping the receiver, his pulse racing in the palm of his hand, wondering whether Tess meant 'you – Liam' or 'you – the whole family'. The French language was much better: there would be a distinction.

'Liam, are you still there?'

'Yes, yeah. I was just thinking, I'm not sure what Josh and Katie are up to this afternoon but—'

'No, I mean just you. I haven't had a chance to talk to you on your own for ages.'

'Yes. Sure. I'm free. Now?'

'Well, finish your lunch. I'll meet you outside The Rose and Crown in half an hour.'

He returned to the kitchen table, feeling flushed.

'Is Tess coming over?' Max asked.

'No. I'm going cycling with her this afternoon – is that OK, Dad?'

'Fine,' said Dad. 'You've got your key. Max has got a doubles match, so, Millie, why don't you and I go to Tesco together?'

'Oh, great,' Millie said sarcastically.

Max was looking at Louis in surprise. 'Where are the two of you going?'

'Dunno,' Louis replied quickly. 'Just around the dales, I guess.'

Max said nothing and started eating again. A few minutes later, Louis washed his plate, shoved on his trainers and grabbed his bike from the barn.

Tess was waiting outside the village pub for him, her hair windswept, her long legs tanned against her bright-blue mountain bike. They set off on the road leading out of the village and for a while cycled side by side in silence, the wind whipping at their cheeks and making their T-shirts billow out behind them. As they picked up speed, curving down the long descent, Louis shouted across, 'Where are we going?'

'You'll see,' Tess replied, and she was smiling.

Fifteen minutes later, after a gruelling, stony uphill struggle that required them to shift right down to their lowest gear, the path narrowed between tall walls of bracken and became so uneven, they were forced to walk. A thin, fine drizzle was now falling from a milky grey sky and Louis was just beginning to wonder what Tess was playing at when he saw, looming high above them in a chiselled mountain of black slate, the vast mouth of a cave. Tess was heading straight for it, her feet scrabbling against the pieces of loose rock; Louis struggled to keep up with her, his calf muscles aching now. As they approached the cave, the rocky path fell away into a pool of clear turquoise water, and Louis saw that there were several large slabs of rock protruding, forming giant stepping stones into the dry part of the cave. Tess threw her bicycle down and began to leap from slab to slab, disappearing towards the vast wall of blackness that stretched up in front of her.

She turned round. 'Come on, Liam!'

Her voice already echoed. Louis put down his bike beside hers and followed her across the stones.

The cave was vast, as high as a house. Drops of water fell from the craggy roof into small pools with an echoing drip. Smaller pieces of rock jutted out from the walls like giant pieces of furniture. Tess jumped off the last stepping stone and walked down the length of the cave, singing, 'O, for the Wings of a Dove'. It was like being in a cathedral with a full choir – the cave resonated with sound. Louis jumped off the last stone and stopped to listen. Her voice was so pure, so clear, he could almost taste it. Tess turned round and broke off, laughing. 'Isn't it great?'

'It's amazing!'

'I come here all the time. When I've had a row with my mum, or just to get some peace after school. Come right to the back – the rock is icy cold.'

She stopped, waiting for him, and he moved forward tentatively.

'Come on!' she said, grabbing his hand. 'It's like we're alone in the whole world.'

Her fingers were cool and firm around his. As they

walked deeper into the cave, it was too dark to read the expression on her face, but he could make out the curve of her forehead, the slant of her nose, the indentation of her chin. At the very back of the cave, Tess lifted Louis' hand and pressed it against the cold, wet rock. 'Turn round,' she whispered.

Louis turned to look back the way they had come. The giants' stepping stones were in the distance, stretching out over the turquoise water. The rain had thickened now, falling against the bright white mouth of sky. A cluster of evergreens stretched up in the distance. It was fairytale.

He turned back to Tess. She was watching him solemnly, very quiet, very still. Suddenly his heart began to pound. Maybe – maybe this was how it sometimes happened? Maybe she was going to kiss *him*?

'You're in the newspaper,' Tess said.

He jerked away in shock. 'What?'

She had already turned, walking swiftly back towards the mouth of the cave. She pulled herself up onto a boulder and motioned him to join her. 'I've got something to show you.'

Adrenaline drunk, he followed and climbed up next to her. She was unfolding a large torn-out piece of newspaper and laying it across his lap.

Louis looked down at it and felt his heart jolt. There was a grainy family photo that had been taken of all five of them on the couch last Christmas. The photo had been divided in two and made to look like it had been savagely ripped: Maman on the one half and Dad and the children on the other. The heading read: A FAMILY TORN APART: MOTHER'S GRIEF AS EX-HUSBAND ABDUCTS THREE CHILDREN. The article went on:

Today, Ms Annette Lombard, mother of three, arrived in London to aid the police in the search for her missing children. 8-year-old Emilie, 12-year-old Louis and 14-year-old Maxime went missing six weeks ago in Paris while spending the weekend with their non-custodial father, Edward Whittaker, who is Irish. He is believed to have brought the three children to England and Ms Lombard has applied for the return of the children to France under the Hague Convention on the Civil Aspects of International Child Abduction. This is the second case of non-custodial abduction between England and France since the establishment of the Hague Convention in 1980, and although the police as yet have no leads, Ms Lombard, who works for a top Paris finance company, is fighting to stay positive. 'It's every mother's worst nightmare. I don't know whether my children are safe or where they are. I know they are with their father, but I am very worried about his mental state. He suffered a major nervous breakdown only last year and is still recovering. Our children have been plucked from their home, their school, their friends and their activities. My daughter, Millie, was due to sit a piano exam last week. My son Louis is a talented dancer and had been entered for a prestigious competition. My son Max has important school exams next term. I am horrified at the selfishness of their father and at his attempt to erase me from our children's lives. I love my children more than anything. I miss them so much. My world has fallen apart.'

Louis looked up from the piece of newspaper and into Tess's serious face. 'It's five days old,' she said. 'I only came across it because I was spreading old newspapers out on the floor to help Mum with the painting. But as soon as I saw the headline, I knew it had to be you lot.'

Louis said nothing and looked back down at the photo; at the ripped photo of his mother now sitting alone.

'What are you going to do with it?' Tess asked softly. 'Are you going to show the others?'

Louis took a deep breath. 'I don't know. Maybe I – maybe I should just—' He brought the sheet of newspaper to his face and pressed it against his eyes.

There was a silence.

'Oh, Louis . . .' Tess said.

He held his breath and didn't move.

He felt Tess's hand on his wrist. 'Give it to me or you'll get it all smudged.' She prised the sheet of newspaper gently from his grasp.

Louis put his hands over his face.

'Louis, I'm sorry, I shouldn't have shown it to you . . .'

He just shook his head, unable to speak, holding his breath to try and stop the tears that spilled down his cheeks, escaping down the backs of his hands through the cracks between his fingers.

Tess rubbed his back. 'Louis, please don't cry,' she said softly. 'Maybe you could call her. Just to say you're all right.'

He felt paralysed with sorrow, disappointment, shame. He wanted her to disappear; he didn't want her to see him cry, but at the same time he wanted her to hug him tight.

'I c-can't,' Louis said raggedly, gasping and sniffing and dragging the sleeves of his sweatshirt viciously down his cheeks. 'It – it would be too risky. If D-Dad got caught, the others would never forgive me.'

'But just because he's wanted by the police doesn't mean your dad will go to prison, surely?' Tess said.

'I mean, it's not as if he's done something awful. You *are* his children.'

'He's b-broken the law,' Louis gasped, wiping his cheeks. Why couldn't he speak normally?

'Wouldn't he just get off with a fine or something?'

'I d-don't know.' Louis sniffed again. 'But Mum would never let us see him again, that's – that's for sure.'

There was another silence. Tess reached over and ruffled Louis' hair. 'Don't cry, dancing boy.'

'I-I'm not.' He pressed his hands to his cheeks and took a long deep breath.

Tess studied him carefully in the low light. 'Are you going to be OK?'

'I *am* OK.' He inhaled and exhaled in carefully measured breaths.

She waited a while. 'So why did your mum get custody anyway?' she asked gently.

'She didn't get sole custody, not initially,' Louis began to explain, struggling to keep his voice even. 'We were staying with her during the week and at Dad's at weekends. But Mum didn't like the arrangement. Dad let us stay up late and took us to places she didn't approve of – they never agreed on anything. Then Mum said she didn't want us going to Dad's for the weekend any more – only for part of the school holidays. And that's when

Dad went a bit crazy. He'd been suffering from depression since the separation, and I guess Mum trying to restrict his access to us just tipped him over the edge. He t-took an overdose of sleeping pills and was in a psychiatric hospital for three months. They said he'd had a nervous breakdown. And while he was in hospital, Mum decided he wasn't responsible enough to look after us on his own any more. So she applied to the courts to have his visitation rights restricted to supervised visits.'

'And she won?' Tess sounded horrified.

Louis inhaled deeply in an attempt to steady himself. 'Yeah. But I only found out the day before Dad took us away. We were staying with him that weekend. He was supposed to break the news to us. It was supposed to be our last weekend with him.'

'And instead of that he bundled you onto a plane and brought you to England.' Tess looked appalled. 'Crikey.'

'It wasn't fair, what she did to him,' Louis said quietly. 'It wasn't fair that she tried to take us away from him.'

A silence. Then, 'But what your dad ended up doing to your mum was even worse,' Tess said.

'I know,' Louis said. 'But he said he didn't have a choice.'

'That's not true,' Tess said. 'People almost always have some kind of choice, however terrible the situation . . .

I'm never getting married,' she declared suddenly, elbowing him in the side. 'I'm going to be like my mum.'

'What did your mum do?' Louis asked.

'Had a kid by herself.'

'You can't do that,' Louis said without thinking.

Tess laughed. 'I don't mean she got pregnant on her own, silly! She just raised me on her own, that's all.'

Louis felt himself blush. 'Oh.'

'Yeah. My dad did a runner when he found out she was pregnant.'

'Did he ever come back?'

'Nope.'

'So you've never met him?'

'No.'

'Have you seen any pictures of him?'

Tess sighed. 'Yeah. A couple. Doesn't look anything like me. Sometimes I wonder if my mum has got the wrong bloke.'

'Do you know his name?'

'Yeah. Damian Salter. Though Mum calls him *that idiot*.'

Louis laughed. Although it hurt his throat, it made him feel slightly better. 'D'you miss not having a dad?'

Tess was thoughtful. 'I don't know. Sometimes, perhaps. Once I saw a man and a little girl coming out of a park together carrying tennis rackets. It made me want to cry. But then again, lots of my friends don't get on with their dads at all. Or else they have dads who don't bother with them. Or who are violent. I think that having no dad is better than having a bad dad.'

'But why don't you want to get married? What if you fall in love?'

Tess looked at him in surprise. 'I don't have to marry him, do I?'

'No, but . . .' He tailed off, embarrassed, and felt himself flush.

Tess looked at him and smiled. 'Ah, you're so sweet,' she said.

Chapter Eleven

For a week Louis kept the newspaper article in his jeans pocket, wondering whether to show it to Max. There was no point in showing Dad, he reckoned – it would only stress him out further. And Dad was *still* stressed, even though they had more or less settled in now. Every afternoon he came home with loads of work, which he saved until after they had gone to bed. And late at night, sometimes in the early hours of the morning, when Louis couldn't sleep, he could make out the light coming from the kitchen and hear the frantic clicking of the computer keyboard.

Louis didn't look at the newspaper article again, although keeping it close in his pocket made him feel closer to Maman somehow. He was relieved that she knew they were safe with Dad, but the last three sentences of the article kept coming back to haunt him: *I love my children more than anything. I miss them so much. My world has fallen apart.* Sometimes, especially late at night, the urge to pick up the phone and just call her was more than he could bear, and the only way to stop himself was to curl his hands into fists and remind himself of the ramifications. The police. Dad arrested. Millie crying. Max shouting. *Dad would kill himself if he ended up in prison*, Louis kept repeating to himself again and again. Maman would not die if she didn't see them for a few years. She would suffer, but she loved her work so much. She loved Charlot, the new man in her life. She would survive.

And then there was Tess. He knew it was selfish, but sometimes Louis had to admit that part of the reason he didn't pick up the phone and call Maman was because of Tess. Going back to France would mean losing her as a friend. And he didn't want that. Not ever. One day he would kiss her. He would. Maybe Max could tell him how it was done. But days passed and Tess did not suggest going back to the cave – though he felt sure she would, sooner or later. And this time he wouldn't let go of her hand. This time he pull her towards him and . . . It was at once too wonderful and too scary to think about.

* * *

The following day, when Dad came home from work, he had news.

'I've enrolled you at a local school,' he told them. 'It's about ten miles away in Coniston, so I'll have to drive you, or there's a bus you can take. But it seems like a really nice place. Meg recommended it to me.'

'School!' Millie's eyes grew wide. 'But I thought we were on holiday!'

'It's August, Millie. School starts again on the fifth of September,' Dad said gently. 'Besides, the sooner you start school, the sooner you'll start sounding like real English children. And you all need some friends your own age . . .'

'Is it a primary *and* secondary school?' Max wanted to know.

'Well, it's a secondary school, but there's a nice little primary school for Millie just across the road.'

'We're gonna have to write in English and stuff?' Max looked worried.

'The school has a learning support centre and it caters well for dyslexics,' Dad replied. 'You'll be allowed to do all your written work on a laptop and you'll be given extra time for exams.'

'Really?' Max looked dumbfounded. 'I can just use the spellchecker the whole time?'

'Absolutely. And there's no system of *redoublement* in this country. So you'll be going into Year Ten with kids your own age.'

'What's Year Ten?'

'*Troisième*.'

Max let out a low whistle.

'You'll have to do those CGE things,' Louis warned him.

'Yes,' Dad replied. 'But you can drop some of the subjects you don't like.'

'What about me? What about me?' Millie crowed.

Dad turned to her. 'You, young lady, will be going into Year Four. Your teacher's name is Mrs Ross, I believe.'

'Do we have to wear uniforms?' Max asked.

'Yes,' Dad said.

'Ooh, gross!' Millie exclaimed. But she was smiling and her eyes were bright.

Dad turned to Louis. 'And you, young man, will be going into Year Eight.'

The day of the competition dawned cloudless and bright. Louis woke up with the familiar popcorn feeling in his chest and started practising straight after breakfast. It was a Saturday and so Dad was at home, minus his laptop for once, drinking coffee while poring over the paper. Millie was overexcited – she loved watching Louis compete – but as a result was leaping about like a jumping bean and getting on everyone's nerves. As Dad tried to persuade her to get dressed, Max was accusing each one of them in turn of having nicked his GameBoy while Louis tried to do triple turns in the small gap between the table and the kitchen sink.

'Aargh! For God's sake!' As Millie pushed past him, he was knocked off-balance and his hip met the sharp corner of the kitchen table. He gripped his side, groaning dramatically.

'Louis, stop practising in here or you're not even going to make it to the competition,' Dad said. 'Millie, how many times do I have to tell you to get dressed?'

'I *am* dressed!' Millie giggled, holding out the hem of her nightie and curtseying. 'This is my princess dress and—'

'If someone doesn't tell me where my GameBoy is right now . . .' Max growled. 'Dad, make them look for it at least!'

'Surely you can go without that gadget for one day—'

'I need it now!' Max shouted. 'I'm not sitting through

a whole bloody dance show without it! Millie, just tell me where you put it. I know you took it – you're always nicking it—'

'Why does everyone always blame me?' Millie sounded outraged as she overfilled her bowl with cereal, sending Coco Pops scattering across the floor.

Dad abandoned his newspaper with a sigh of exasperation. 'Millie, I want you to get dressed *before* you have your breakfast—'

'Dad, make her find my GameBoy first!'

'I don't have it! How many times do I have to tell you!'

'You're lying!'

'Ow!' Millie had got too close to Louis' *fouettés* and his foot met with her eye. She staggered backwards, howling dramatically. 'I'm blinded! He blinded me!'

'Right, that's it!' Dad shouted. 'Everyone upstairs! You can wait there till it's time to leave!'

When they finally got into the car, some sort of truce had been achieved. Max was still scowling about the loss of his GameBoy; Millie was still wearing a pained expression; Louis was gnawing on his thumbnail. Tess had rung last night to tell them her mother was holed up in bed with stomach flu and wouldn't be able to make it, so they picked Tess up in the village and arrived outside Preston leisure centre in time to meet Miss Kano in the car park. Tess's eyes were very bright and she jumped up and down and grabbed Louis' arm and gripped it very tightly. Miss Kano and Dad chatted for a bit, and then Dad took Max and Millie off to get ice creams while Miss Kano led them into the building. After going into their respective changing rooms to put on their costumes, they reconvened in the waiting hall that resonated with the roar of excited chatter. There were kids everywhere: milling about, sitting in groups with their dance teachers or parents, stretching or practising elements from their routines.

Miss Kano found them a small space in a corner and Louis and Tess sat down and drank from their water bottles and ate their energy bars while Miss Kano went off to the front of the room to register them.

Louis looked up at Tess as she adjusted the straps of her leotard. 'Nervous?'

'Terrified,' she replied, but she was grinning.

Miss Kano returned with their numbers, which she pinned to their backs. Because their dance was mainly modern, they had gone for street costumes: Tess wore a stretchy denim miniskirt over a black leotard and Louis wore stretchy jeans and a white tank top with NEW YORK emblazoned on it and Max's black sweatband round his wrist. But some of the kids around looked like show ponies – with tassels and make-up and even bells!

Then there was a long wait. They did some gentle warm-up exercises, watching the board anxiously for their numbers. Louis glanced up at the clock and hoped that Dad, Max and Millie had taken their seats in the main sports hall. Then, suddenly, a number was called out and Tess was grabbing his arm, her eyes wide. 'That's us!'

Miss Kano was getting to her feet, an encouraging smile on her face. 'OK. Deep breaths. Remember your timings.'

She followed them to the door and wished them luck. Then she disappeared to take her seat in the main hall and Louis and Tess were left alone.

'We'll just do our best,' Tess was saying, gripping Louis' hand, her breathing fast and shallow. 'That's all we can do, right?'

'We'll be fine, Tess,' Louis said, with more conviction than he felt. 'We'll be fine.'

They were led into the vast sports hall and the audience on the packed bleachers burst into applause. They gave their names and numbers to the three judges sitting behind the trestle tables and Louis tried to avert his eyes from Dad, Max and Millie, who were sitting in the front row. A final squeeze of Tess's hand and then they were taking up their positions on the mark in the centre of the hall, back to back – the simple starting positions they had come up with just a few weeks ago. There was a moment's deafening silence. And then the music began.

Afterwards, it was hard to remember performing the actual routine. It all seemed to go very quickly. Louis remembered hoping his knees weren't shaking visibly as he stood ready to begin. But once the dance started, there was no time to think about anything. The adrenaline pumping through his body made even the tumbling feel effortless. The slower moves were harder, though, especially the ones that required careful balance. He remembered thinking that the music was very loud and that Tess's eyes were very bright. He messed up the timing on the *fouettés* and only just managed to stop at the same time as Tess; then got too close to her on the backwards walkovers and felt her hand push against his arm. But there were no disasters. And when they returned to their back-to-back position for the finish, the applause and wolf-whistles from the stands were deafening.

Back in the waiting hall, they couldn't stop talking,

rehashing every move with Miss Kano at the top of their voices. Eventually they calmed down, downed a bottle of water each, got changed and went to meet the others in the car park.

'You were the best! You were the best!' Millie was squealing and jumping up and down with excitement.

Max shot Louis a grin and said, 'Yeah, not bad.'

Dad put his hand on Louis' shoulder and said, 'Well done, son. That was terrific. I felt very proud.'

They all went out for a pizza together. The results wouldn't be announced till two and so there was a good hour to wait. In the restaurant, Miss Kano talked about the next round in London. Only the winners of this round would get to go. 'But even if you're a runner-up, there's still a cash prize.'

'I think you're going to win, I think you're going to win!' Millie exclaimed excitedly.

'Steady on, Katie,' Miss Kano said with a smile. 'They did really well but there were some other fabulous dancers too. We'll just have to wait and see what the judges decide.'

Tess caught Louis' eye across the table. 'But whatever the outcome, our dance was the best, wasn't it?' She grinned.

Louis nodded. 'Absolutely.'

Back in the stands, the tension was palpable. At the end of the hall, the three judges stood behind the trestle tables on which were displayed an array of medals. There was a long and boring speech by one of the organizers about the different forms of dance and the nature of competition and how every contestant was a winner, etc. Then came the announcements.

'Third place goes to Anna Jenkins and Simon Williams.'

A round of applause. Two teenagers came out to collect their medals, beaming and looking back at their friends.

'Second place goes to Alisha Kuwa and Tyrone Pierce.'

More clapping. Louis recognized two talented street-dancers he'd noticed warming up outside before the competition.

Tess gave him an agonized look, biting her lower lip. Louis found himself holding his breath.

'And first place goes to Tess Morham and Liam Franklin.'

Deafening applause. It took Louis a moment to react. He recognized Tess's name but not his own. But then Miss Kano's hands were on his shoulders, propelling him forward, and Tess was grabbing his hand, gasping in disbelief.

Dazed, Louis followed her towards the judges' table, where they received their medals. There were backslaps and flowers and handshakes, and Louis and Tess were asked what it felt like to have won and whether they were excited at the prospect of competing in the next round in London. Millie hugged them each tightly round the waist, and Max ruffled Louis' hair and gave Tess a kiss on the cheek, which made her blush. More strangers came up to ask further questions and Louis and Tess were asked to pose for a photo, but as soon as the flash went off, Dad's mood suddenly changed. He grabbed Louis by the arm and ordered them all into the car. In the car park, Louis rolled down the window, and he and Tess called out their thanks to Miss Kano, promising to start thinking about music for the London heats. But Dad just gunned the engine and they roared off home.

As soon as they reached the farmhouse, Tess called her mum to tell her the news while Dad started preparing things for dinner. Louis was on a high, doing handstands and walkovers in the courtyard, adrenaline-drunk from their wonderful day. Millie paraded around with his gold medal hanging from her neck and even Max seemed cheerful. They would be competing in London in September, Louis kept on thinking. Could they win that round too? Then they would be only one stage away from the Royal Variety Show!

But Dad seemed to be simmering about something. He snapped at Millie to feed her cat and told Louis to lay the table. Millie returned, complaining that Treasure was nowhere to be found. Dad turned from the cooker and said, 'Josh, go and help Katie bring her cat inside, will you?'

'I'll go,' said Tess.

Louis finished laying the table and helped Dad dish up. His arms and legs were beginning to ache with exhaustion but his chest was bursting with a feeling of complete elation.

'Dad, I can't wait for the next round of the competition! Do you think we might win that too?'

Dad said nothing. Perhaps he hadn't heard. He finished dishing up the spaghetti bolognese and then looked round in annoyance. 'Where the hell is everyone?'

'Looking for Treasure, I think.'

'Then go and call them, will you? It's going to get cold.'

Louis went out into the courtyard. He met Millie walking up the dirt track with Treasure in her arms. 'Dinner's ready,' Louis told her. 'Where are the others?'

'In the barn.'

Louis crossed the courtyard and scraped open the corrugated-iron door.

'Dinner's—' He broke off, frozen. There, in a shaft of warm evening sunlight, Max and Tess stood with their arms around each other, kissing.

Chapter Twelve

Monday morning, Dad didn't go to work. Louis woke to hear the sound of cupboard doors slamming and china plates clattering from the kitchen below. Max and Millie were already up – Millie was buttering a large slice of toast and talking to her cat; Max had his feet up on a chair, reading a magazine between spoonfuls of cereal.

'Are you still eating?' Dad barked at Max as Louis took a seat at the table.

'No, Dad, I'm just pretending to eat,' Max retorted. 'This chewing motion I'm doing is just a form of exercise for my jaw—'

'That's enough,' Dad snapped. 'Put the comic down and hurry up with your breakfast.'

'Why?' Max lowered the magazine and looked up in

disbelief. 'You know, Dad, it is sometimes actually possible to do more than one thing at a time.'

'I need to drive into town and sort some things out. I want you to finish breakfast so you can come with me.'

'Oh, Daaad . . .' Millie put down her toast and rolled her eyes dramatically.

'I'm not coming with you,' Max stated. 'I've got a doubles match with Ned at twelve.'

'Cancel it,' Dad snapped.

'No!' Max exclaimed, outraged. 'Why should I?'

Dad gave him one of his warning looks. 'Just do as you're told, Max, OK?'

Max gave Dad a furious glare, threw his spoon down on the table and stalked over to the telephone. Dad picked up Max's bowl, put it in the sink and started wiping the table.

'Daaad . . .' Millie complained as he lifted her plate to wipe beneath it.

'Come on, Millie, you're too slow. Where are your shoes? You haven't even brushed your hair.'

'I haven't finished my toast!'

Louis broke off a small piece of croissant and put it in his mouth.

After muttering darkly on the phone for several minutes, Max replaced the receiver with a crash and turned to Dad. 'Thanks a lot for ruining my day.'

'Put on your shoes and get in the car,' Dad said, ignoring the comment. 'Are you ready, Louis?'

'Yeah,' Louis said.

Getting into the car with the others, Louis felt numb. His arms and legs no longer seemed to belong to him; he was moving on autopilot, just putting one foot in front of the other, going through the motions. As Max and Millie squabbled for the front seat, as Dad shouted at them both and relegated them all to the back, Louis tried to focus on doing the things that were expected of him and concentrated on not falling apart. But a sharp sliver of pain seemed to have lodged itself deep inside his chest and it hurt to be alive. There was a constant burn at the back of his throat, an ache behind his eyes, a weakness in his arms and legs and a feeling of sadness – of sadness so strong, he had to take rapid shallow breaths to control it. It was a pain he had never experienced before – like missing someone so much you thought you were going to die. Tess . . .

Last night he had wanted to sob her name into his pillow, but had held his breath and stemmed the tears for fear that Max would hear. And now he had to somehow get through another whole day without anyone guessing what was wrong. How Max would laugh if he knew. And he could just imagine the pitying look on Dad's face and the gentle words: *Oh, Louis, you couldn't have thought she was interested in you! You're only a child. She's fourteen! She thinks of you as her little brother*.

By the time they reached the town, Dad and Max were arguing again. 'Why the hell did you make us come with you if you just wanted to leave us locked up in the car?' Max was shouting.

'I didn't want to leave you at home on your own today,' Dad was saying. 'For once in your life, Max, just do as you're told without arguing, OK?'

'No, it's not OK! I'm getting out of the car and looking round the shops if you're going to the bank! It's boiling in this car and I don't see why I should stay here just because it's more convenient for you!' They went on and on as Dad circled the busy car park, searching for a space.

Louis kept his cheek pressed to the window, staring out blindly. He felt the touch of a hand on his arm. 'Loulou?'

'Mm.'

'What are you thinking about?' Millie asked.

'Nothing.' He didn't turn round.

'Why is Dad being so angry?'

'Dunno.'

After being cooped up in the car for half an hour while Dad ran his errands, tempers had reached boiling point and Max and Millie were locked in another furious row over who got to sit in the front. Dad slammed back into the driving seat with a handful of papers that he threw across the dashboard, started the engine and shot the car forward with a furious jerk. Millie, who'd lost the front-seat war and hadn't got her seatbelt on, smacked her forehead on the headrest in front and promptly burst into tears. Max, who thought she was crying because of the seating arrangements, twisted round and said, 'God, you can really be such a baby—'

'Shut up!' Dad suddenly yelled. 'Shut up, the lot of you! I've had enough of your complaints and endless squabbling! You're just spoiled, ungrateful brats! You have no idea how much *work* has gone into bringing you to England with me! I don't know why I ever bothered!'

There was a terrible silence. Louis saw that Dad's face was bright red. Beads of perspiration had broken out in the crevasses that lined his forehead. Louis had never heard him shout like that before. Even Max had flinched.

Louis leaned over and pulled Millie's seatbelt across her as she sat, eyes wide, looking stricken. Max swore under his breath and rolled down the window, leaning his chin on his arm and glaring out.

Millie choked back a whimper and said, 'Louis didn't do anything, Daddy.'

Dad drove on in silence, his jaw set. Millie took a deep breath to say something else and Louis gave her a quick shake of the head. She remained silent.

Back at the farmhouse they got out of the car in the worst silence imaginable. Millie was still crying silently, now and again letting out small, muffled, whimpering noises which only added to the tension. Max headed straight for the barn and grabbed his bike, but Dad stopped him. 'Where d'you think you're going?'

'Anywhere,' Max muttered. 'As far away from here as possible.'

'Come inside the house. I need to talk to you.'

'No,' Max said.

Millie cringed and Louis braced himself for another volley of shouting, but Dad just said, 'Come inside, all of you,' in such a flat, defeated voice that Max put down his bike and followed him in without another word.

They sat around the kitchen table, looking glum. Millie was still sniffing. Max was still glowering. Louis stared blankly at a stain on the table where Millie had once spilled some ketchup. Dad sat down heavily and took a deep breath. 'I'm very, very sorry I shouted at you all in the car just now,' he said, his voice low and oddly subdued. 'I lost my temper and I didn't mean what I said. I'm just very angry right now. Not at you. I should have never taken it out on you.'

Millie instantly brightened, suddenly realizing that no telling-off was forthcoming. 'Who are you angry at, Daddy?'

'I'm angry at Miss Kano,' Dad replied.

Louis' head snapped up. 'What?'

Even Max looked interested. 'Is this about the competition?'

'Yes,' Dad replied. He took another breath. 'Miss Kano assured me there would be no press present at the dance competition on Saturday. I expressly told her that we were a camera-shy family and didn't want our picture to appear in any kind of publication.'

'In case we were recognized,' Max said.

'Exactly – though of course I didn't tell her that. Well, the damn woman completely let me down.' Dad got up and, with an angry sigh, yanked open a kitchen drawer and pulled out a newspaper. 'It's only the local rag, but look at this,' he said.

He threw the paper down on the table. Max and Millie instantly grabbed at it. Max won the fight and

Millie climbed onto the table to get a better look. With a shaky feeling in his limbs, Louis got up and stood behind Max.

NEWCOMER TRIUMPHS AT JUNIOR DANCE COMPETITION

There was a grinning picture of Louis and Tess, holding up their medals to the camera. Below it, the article read:

Twelve-year-old Liam Franklin, from Grasmere, hasn't been in the country very long but already he's started making a name for himself by winning first prize at the Junior Modern-Dance Competition yesterday in Preston, with his dance partner, Tess Morham. The Franklin family – dad Jonathan, sister Katie (8) and brother Josh (14) – moved into one of the refurbished holiday homes near Grasmere after moving here all the way from New Caledonia just two months ago. And according to Liam's dance teacher, Mrs Asha Kano, Liam is already showing tremendous promise as a dancer. 'I can't take all the credit because I've only had him in my class for four weeks,' the Windermere-based Miss Kano said. 'For someone so young, he is already showing incredible maturity in his interpretation and expression. He is one of those rare dancers who is able to combine all forms of movement, from ballet to street-dance to gymnastics, and move across all styles seamlessly.'

Max was the first to speak. 'Oh, no,' he breathed.

'What does "seamlessly" mean?' Millie wanted to know.

'Shut up, Millie, that's not important,' Max said. 'Dad, what are we going to do?'

'What *can* we do?' Dad said. 'Except just lie low and keep our fingers crossed.'

'Are we going to have to move?' Max asked.

'Oh no, oh no, please no!' Millie begged.

'Hopefully not,' Dad said. 'But for the next few days we're going to have to be very, very careful. That's why I took the day off work today. That's why I didn't want you going off on your own. Hopefully this story will just get buried and no one will give it another thought. But we must keep our heads down for the next few days, just in case.'

'So we can't leave the house?' Millie asked, her eyes wide.

'We can,' said Dad. 'We'll have to, but together. I don't want us to get separated in case we have to make a sudden getaway. It's important we're still seen around and just keep to our normal business. I've said I'm working at home this week – just to be on the safe side.'

'Why did Miss Kano lie to you about the press?' Max asked.

'I've no idea,' Dad said. 'But Louis, listen. I'm afraid that's the end of any more dance classes, and the competition in London is obviously out of the question. We can't have anything to do with that woman again.'

Louis stared up at his father in horror. 'Dad, no! She didn't do this on purpose – she wasn't to know!'

'Louis, I'm not even going to discuss this with you now. Our house, our whole life here is in jeopardy because of that woman. We can't trust her and we can't risk you going to competitions again and having your photo in the paper. You'll have to do your dancing at home.'

Louis felt the heat rush to his face and it was a monumental effort not to shout. 'Dad, you can't ban me from dance classes! It's what I love more than anything! It's what I do best!'

'Oh, for goodness' sake, Louis, stop being so dramatic,' Max pitched in. 'It's not like there's a career to being a dancer or anything—'

'How do you know?' Louis found himself shouting

now. 'You don't know the first thing about dancing! Miss Kano said I was good enough to go on the West End stage. They are holding auditions down in Leeds for the musical *Billy Elliot* – she said that I'd have an excellent chance—!'

'Louis, you should have known that would be completely out of the question,' Dad said. 'There's no way you could appear on stage while we're wanted by the police—'

'*You're* the one who's wanted by the police!' Louis yelled. '*You're* the one who broke the law! Why should *we* have to pay the price?' He could feel the blood pounding in his cheeks, feel the shouts tear at his throat. He knew he was being unreasonable, demanding, vain even. But he didn't care. Suddenly the pain of having the two things he cared about most, brutally and unfairly snatched from his grasp, was too much to bear. Two days ago he had been so happy, so excited. And now—

'Louis, I'm sorry,' Dad said. 'But that's just the way it is. We made a joint decision to stay here. And we knew there would be sacrifices. I'm just sorry this had to be the first.' He rubbed the back of his hand across his eyes, looking exhausted, and moved towards the kitchen door. 'I'm going upstairs to call Meg,' he said quietly. 'Please don't leave the house without me. I really need your co-operation and support if we're to get through this together.' And with that, he left the room.

Louis sank down on a kitchen chair, breathing heavily. His heart was thumping so hard his whole chest hurt. He found that his hands were shaking and pressed them together to try to stop it. He felt suffocated, chained to the house, buried alive. He couldn't understand why the others didn't feel it too.

Max looked at him with a patronizing air. 'God, you really know how to make things worse, don't you.'

Louis didn't look at him, hands still clenched together in his lap. 'Don't even start, Max . . .' His voice shook.

Millie picked up Treasure and retreated warily to a corner of the room.

'Don't even start what?' Max demanded, his eyes narrowing. 'I can't believe you were such a baby about your precious dance classes. Don't you think we've all got more important stuff to be worrying about?'

Louis looked slowly up at him. 'Get lost,' he said.

Max stepped forward, his eyes narrowing. 'What?'

'I'm sure *you've* got more important stuff to be worrying about,' Louis repeated. 'Like your new girlfriend, for example.'

Max's cheeks flared. 'How do you know?'

'I saw you in the barn!'

Max's eyes filled with scorn. 'Don't tell me you're jealous!'

'She's my friend!'

'Yes, *friend*,' Max repeated, almost spitting out the word. 'That's it, just *friends*. There's no law saying I can't go out with other people's friends, is there?'

'You knew I liked her!'

'You're twelve years old! Tess is nearly fifteen. Did you think there was any chance she would go out with a *child*?'

'I'm not a child!' Louis yelled, leaping to his feet, his chair clattering to the floor.

'Look' – Max held out his hands – 'what was I supposed to say – *oh, I'm sorry, I can't go out with you because my kid brother has a crush on you?*'

'She was *my* friend!'

'Listen to yourself! You're twelve going on six!'

Louis' arm started moving before he had time to think. His knuckles made contact with Max's jaw and he heard Millie scream. Suddenly his clenched fist was throbbing and Max was lying on the floor. He turned and ran from the room.

Louis heard the barn door scrape open. He didn't move. Sitting on the cold stone floor against the wall, knees drawn up, hands over his face, he could feel the hot tears trickling down between his fingers, down the inside of his wrists. Shuffling footsteps approached, then a small voice said, 'Louis?'

He didn't look up. Held his breath and hoped she would go away. But her arm brushed against his leg as she sat down beside him, and he felt the press of her small body against his shoulder.

'Loulou . . .'

He took a shuddering breath, trying to keep the sound of tears from his voice. 'Just leave me alone.'

There was a silence. Then Millie said, 'I don't like Max either.'

Louis sniffed hard and said nothing.

'Loulou?'

'What?'

'Are you sad because Tess is Max's girlfriend now?'

He didn't reply.

'I think she made a mistake,' Millie said. 'I think she's really silly. She just likes Max because he's the oldest. But you're the nicest.'

A muffled sob escaped him. He bit his tongue hard.

'Louis, please don't cry,' Millie went on, her voice very small.

He tried to oblige, holding his breath again.

'You're *my* favourite,' Millie said. 'You're the best brother in the whole world.'

Louis breathed deeply, trying to stem the tears. 'I'm just really sick of this—'

'Sick of Max?'

'No, sick of this. Having to hide, having to change our names, having to pretend we're someone else.' He sniffed again. 'It might have been fun for a few weeks but it's wearing a bit thin now.'

'But wouldn't you rather live with Dad than with Maman?' Millie asked, sounding surprised.

'I don't know any more,' Louis said, and he put his hands back over his face and started to sob – for a mother he'd lost, for a stolen girl he'd never even had a chance with, for a dancing career that was over before it had even begun.

Chapter Thirteen

The week that followed was one of the longest of Louis'
life. Dad was trying to work from home, but he was tense
and snappy. Louis and Max had entered a cold war, and
weren't talking to each other except when strictly
necessary. Millie was the only one who seemed happy,
spending her time reading and sunbathing and playing
with her cat. Despite the purple bruise on Max's jaw,
Dad hadn't said anything about Louis' punch – perhaps
because he had other things on his mind, or perhaps
because he understood. Tess came round to dinner a
couple of times, but there was no dance practice as Dad
had told Louis to pretend to Miss Kano he had hurt his
leg. After the meal Max and Tess would disappear
upstairs together. The pain Louis felt when he glanced
across the kitchen table at her was almost too much to

bear – she was still friendly towards him, but he saw now that it was in the same way as she was friendly towards Millie – like an older sister.

The following Monday, Dad went back to work. He had a big presentation to give in the afternoon which he couldn't miss, and he seemed to have finally relaxed about the newspaper article. Max and Millie went swimming in the lake mid-morning while Louis stayed at home watching TV. A dull, heavy apathy seemed to have encased him so that even the clear blue sky and glassy lakes had lost their appeal. He felt hollow, numb and useless. When Max and Millie returned for lunch, flushed from the ride, brown from the sun, hair still dripping, their loud voices and good cheer were exhausting. Max put some pasta on to cook and asked Louis if he was hungry, Millie laid the table talking about a baby deer they'd seen swimming in the water, and Louis did his best to join in, not wanting to appear as if he was still sulking.

'And the baby deer was swimming doggy-paddle, like this!' Millie was saying, doing a rather good impression of a deer trying to keep its head above water. 'And it was turning its head this way and that way. It was so cute, Louis, you should have come! I wished I could have taken it home. D'you think deers can be kept as pets? Like if we built a fence round the garden—'

'They're wild animals,' Louis said. 'It would be cruel.'

'They say that deer meat is very tender,' Max said, dishing up the pasta with an evil laugh.

'Oh, horrid!' Millie exclaimed.

'You've never eaten deer meat,' Louis said to Max.

'No, but I *have* eaten horse. And I must say it was pretty good.'

'No!' Millie cried in horror. 'How could you, Max? That's so cruel!'

'Well, it was already dead,' Max said from around a mouthful of pasta. 'So what difference did it make whether I ate it or not?'

'When did you eat horse meat?' Louis asked him suspiciously.

'When we went to stay with *Grandmère* in Port Camargue, the year before she died,' Max replied. 'You were there too. You ate it too.'

'That's only because I was too young to know what I was eating,' Louis retorted.

'What difference does it make?' Max asked. 'We eat pigs and chickens on a regular basis. Are horses or deer somehow more important?'

'No,' Louis said. 'They're just more beautiful.'

'I'm going to be vegetarian when I grow up,' Millie

announced. 'That way I won't be eating *any* poor animals.'

'It won't make any difference,' Max said. 'There'll still be just as many dead chickens in the supermarkets.'

'So?' Millie retorted. 'At least it won't be me that's eating them!'

'Why not become a vegetarian right now?' Louis said. 'Why wait till you're grown up?'

'Louis!' Max exclaimed. 'Stop putting ideas in her head!'

'I'm not,' Louis countered. 'She's the one who came up with idea of—'

'I can't be a vegetarian yet,' Millie said sensibly. 'I'm still growing. I need protein for my bones, and anyway, I hardly ever eat meat.'

'You're eating meat now,' Max told her.

'Aargh!' She spat her mouthful onto her plate.

'Millie!' Max and Louis yelled at her in unison.

'You're disgusting,' Max said.

'Clear it up,' said Louis.

'He said I was eating meat!'

'You eat meat all the time!' Louis shouted at her. 'Anyway, Max is lying, there's no meat in pasta.'

'What are those white bits then?'

'Cheese!'

'Well, cheese comes from an animal, doesn't it? So if I'm going to become a vegetarian, I shouldn't—'

Suddenly, outside the kitchen window, there was a scrabbling of loose stones and a frantic thudding on the front door.

Max dropped his fork and stared at Louis, his eyes wide. Millie drew in her breath sharply.

'Don't move,' Louis said. 'Don't move. Don't make a sound.'

'Is it the police?' Millie whimpered.

'Shh,' Max said to her.

They sat, frozen, round their plates of half-eaten pasta. The thudding came again, this time louder.

'Please open the door!' they heard a voice call. 'It's me, Tess!'

Max let out a sigh of relief. Louis picked up his fork again, his heart still thudding. Millie leaped from her seat and ran out into the hall.

But when Millie returned with Tess, Max jumped up. 'What's happened?'

Her face was streaked with tears. Her hair was wild and windswept and she was panting so hard she looked ready to collapse. 'You've got to go,' she gasped. 'Please. You've got to go, now. They know. They all know.'

'What are you talking about?' Max was pulling out a

chair and pushing her down into it. 'Katie, get me a glass of water. Tess, just calm down. Try and catch your breath.'

But Tess was still trying to speak, pushing Max's arm away. 'Louis,' she said desperately, 'they know.'

Louis hadn't moved from his place at the table, his fork still in his hand. He stared at Tess, feeling the blood drain from his face and a cold shiver of horror spread over his skin. 'You promised—' he whispered.

'Would somebody tell me what the hell is going on?' Max shouted, his eyes wide with outrage. 'Who knows what? What on earth are you talking about?'

Louis got up from the table and backed away, staring at Max, his hands beginning to shake. 'I told her,' he said.

'Told her *what*?' Max was looking daggers at Louis, as if still trying to pretend there was nothing to tell.

'Everything,' Louis whispered.

Max turned back to Tess, his eyes widening in horror. She nodded, biting back a sob.

'Oh my God.' Max stared at Louis. 'Oh my God, you stupid, stupid idiot—'

He stepped forward and Louis staggered back, crashing into the saucepan rack.

'Stop it!' Tess jumped up and stood in front of Max.

'Stop it – there's no time to lose, you've got to get out of here—!' She was sobbing, clawing at Max's arm.

Max put his arm tightly around her. 'This is all your fault,' he hissed at Louis. 'All your fault. If Dad gets arrested for this, I'll never forgive you for as long as I live.'

Louis felt a pain start up at the back of his throat. He looked at Tess. 'You promised . . .' was all he could say.

Tess shook her head, tears running down her cheeks. 'I'm sorry, I'm so sorry. I wrote about it in my diary. And my stupid, snooping mum—!'

'Right, come on, we've got to think fast.' Max gripped the top of Tess's arms and turned her round to face him. 'Who knows, exactly?'

'My mum,' Tess gasped. 'And she was on the phone to the police when I ran out of the house.'

Max paled. 'How long ago was that?'

'Fifteen, twenty minutes—'

'OK,' Max said, his voice shaking. 'It's all right, we've got time. You go home. The police will probably come round and interview you and your mum. You've got to try and get the diary off her and burn it. Then you've got to tell the police that it was all a lie, that it was just a story you made up for fun, OK?'

'OK.' Tess gasped and nodded.

'Go now.'

'Max?'

'Yes?'

'Will I ever see you again?'

'Of course,' Max said. 'I'll be in touch as soon as we've got away. We'll find a way to keep seeing each other, I promise.' He kissed her, hard, on the mouth.

Louis turned away.

As soon as Tess had left, Max grabbed the phone to call Dad. Louis went in pursuit of Millie, who was running through the house. 'I have to find Treasure—!'

'You can't take him, Millie.'

She turned to him, stricken, her eyes filling with tears. 'But he's my cat! I'm not leaving without him!'

Louis gripped his sister by the arms, fighting to stay calm. 'Listen, Millie. We can't go and find Treasure, we haven't got time. Besides, we'd have to put him in a bag and he'd be really scared. We have to leave now, d'you understand? Otherwise we're going to get caught and Dad will be arrested. Treasure will be all right. We'll ask Tess to look after him.'

Millie screwed up her eyes as if attempting to shut out the world around her.

'Go and put on your shoes,' he told her. 'Then wait for me and Max at the front door.'

Back in the kitchen, Max slammed down the receiver, breathing hard. 'It keeps going straight to answerphone! Either he's got no reception or he's switched the bloody thing off! What the hell are we going to do now?'

Louis clenched his hands into fists, trying desperately to think. His ears strained for the sound of distant sirens.

'We need to leave the house as quickly as possible,' he said. 'The first place the police will look is here.'

'But what about Dad?'

'We'll find a way of reaching him once we've left,' Louis said. 'But first we need to try and think of what we need to take. We need a rucksack.'

They raced upstairs and Max went to get his rucksack while Louis turned Dad's bedroom upside down. He emptied drawers and cupboards until he found what he was looking for – a shoebox full of passports, papers, ID and other documents. He would just have to pray it was all there. Max ran in with his rucksack and Louis shoved the lot inside and zipped it up. Then he swung it onto his back.

'Anything else?' Max gasped.

'Can't think. Let's go.'

'Dad's laptop? It might have important stuff on it!'

'Have we got another rucksack?'

'Yours. I'll get it.'

Minutes later they were standing outside the farm-house. Millie had pulled herself together, but her eyes were huge, her face white, terrified. Max locked up the house while Louis scanned the road at the far end of the dirt track for any sign of a police car. 'Bikes,' he said. 'We shouldn't go down the dirt track – they could cut us off.'

'Up Easedale?' Max gasped as they ran for the barn.

'Too bare. We'll be seen. Let's head for the wood.'

They grabbed their bikes and set off away from the track, in the opposite direction to the village, across the grass and up the narrow path that snaked its way around the dales. The ferns and bracken were over-grown here, creating a dense green tunnel, but the path was stony and relentlessly uphill. Max led the way and Louis brought up the rear, urging Millie to try and go faster. 'Come on, Millie! Push, push! Come on, come on, you can do it, I know you can do it!'

But Millie's gasps were laced with whimpers and she let out a small, frantic cry whenever the wheel of her bike bounced against a stone. Louis stood up on his pedals to try and get up some speed, the heavy rucksack weighing down his bike as it skidded and slithered over the uneven path. They met a group of hikers, who stood back and watched them shoot past with a look of surprise.

Millie's sobs were audible now. 'I can't go any further. My legs are hurting so much I'm going to die!'

'Come on!' Louis said desperately. 'We're nearly there, we're nearly there. Look up – can you see the forest? It's only another mile . . .'

'I can't, Louis. I can't do it. I can't breathe . . .'

'Keep going, keep going,' Louis urged her. 'Max, slow down, for Christ's sake!'

As soon as they reached the edge of the wood, the air turned cool, damp and eerily still. The wheels of their bikes juddered over the gnarly roots and twigs, the sound of Millie's rasping breath magnified in the still air. When Louis and Max decided they had gone in deep enough, they buried their bikes and bags in a tangled clump of undergrowth and looked about wildly for a climbable tree. There weren't any.

'What about this one?' Louis panted, pointing.

'No way!' Max exclaimed.

'I can give you a leg up,' Louis gasped. 'You'd be able to reach that lowest branch.'

'S'pose we could try . . .'

Louis leaned forward, bracing his shoulder against the tree trunk, legs apart, hands on his knees. He felt the sole of Max's shoe against his spine.

'Ready?'

'Yeah.'

The shoe suddenly became a pillar of weight, crushing down on his back. Louis staggered and heard Max gasp as he grabbed hold of the branch. There was the sound of scrabbling and then the weight disappeared. Louis stood up. Max was straddling the branch, its leaves shaking ominously. He leaned forward to lie on his front and reached a hand down for Millie.

Millie was shivering, her teeth chattering loudly. 'I can't do it, it's too high,' she gasped.

'Yes you can,' Louis said firmly. 'Stand with your legs apart.'

She did as she was told and Louis got down on his knees and put his head between her legs. Bracing himself against the tree trunk, he raised himself up onto one knee. Then, with every muscle screaming, he fought his way up to a standing position. With Millie now seated on his shoulders, he swayed for a moment, almost losing his balance, then managed to stagger close enough to the branch so that she was able to reach it with her hands. He shouted at her to stand up on his shoulders and, with Max's help, she scrambled up.

Max helped her crawl across the branch and huddle into the fork of the tree. Then he looked down at Louis. 'How the hell are *you* going to get up?'

Louis staggered back, craning his neck to look up at them, his knees weak. 'I'm going to get Dad.'

'How? Where?'

'I'll cycle into Windermere. You two stay here for half an hour. Then come out of the other side of the wood and go down the hill towards the main road. Dad and I will pick you up at the fork in the road by the church.'

'When exactly?'

Louis checked his watch. 'At three o'clock. Start cycling down at quarter to. Wait for us behind the hedgerow beside the church. Find somewhere to ditch the bikes. But whatever you do, don't forget the rucksacks.'

Louis bent down to retrieve his bike from the undergrowth.

'Wait,' Max said. 'What if you get caught?'

'I won't,' Louis said, with a great deal more conviction than he felt.

'Three o'clock then,' Max said. Suddenly, he looked as frightened as Millie.

'Three o'clock at the church.' Louis straddled his bike and pushed away.

Freed from the heavy rucksacks and now on a down-hill slope, he was soon able to pick up speed, the wheels of his bike raking up the damp earth. He was afraid of getting lost in the wood, afraid of going round in circles, but knew that if he carried on in a straight line, going in the opposite direction from the way they had come, he would eventually have to emerge from the other side and should find himself above the main road. But time was running out. Perhaps he was already too late. If this had been a normal day, Dad would have gone home by now. But today he had that important presentation . . .

Erupting from the wood into brilliant sunlight, Louis slammed on his brakes and skidded to a halt. From here, looking out round the curve of the mountain, he could just make out the farmhouse and the thin wisp of dirt track leading up to it. At first the track looked empty, but as Louis' eyes followed it up towards the farmhouse, he saw something that made him gasp. A car was parked in front. From this distance, he couldn't make out the markings on the car, but he recognized the small domed shape on the top. It was a police car. Louis felt himself start to shake. How long till the police looked through the kitchen window at the half-eaten pasta and realized they had done a runner? How long till they met the group of hikers coming down from Easedale and asked them whether they had seen three kids running away? How long till the hikers pointed the police in the direction of the wood? Louis looked wildly around him.

The hikers' trail followed the side of the wood and then curved gently downwards towards the bottom of the mountain, but there was no time to follow that route. Here, out of the wood, he was bare and exposed. The police only had to look through a pair of binoculars to see a boy on a bicycle weaving his way down the side of the mountain. No, he had to get down as quickly as possible and disappear amongst the cars that dotted the main road. And the only way to do that was to go straight down the side. The thin curve of grey tarmac stretched out beneath him, snaking its way round the foothills, matchbox cars following it along. He toyed with the idea of sending his bike down on its own and then sliding down after it, but realized that if he broke the bike, the plan was finished. It seemed like the only obvious thing to do was go down the steep grassy mountainside *on* his bike. But the thought of it made his insides twist and clench with fear.

He positioned the bike, took a deep breath, and edged the front wheel forward, adrenaline pumping full throttle. One foot skimming the ground for balance, he began his descent, his knuckles white around the brakes. The first fifty metres or so weren't too bad – the grass was thick and he was able to dig his wheels in and use his foot to take the edge off his speed. He was never fully in control from the start – his descent was too rapid for that – but he could just make out some rocks jutting out from the hillside and he managed to keep them well to his left. Then the ground beneath his wheels began to harden and he could feel himself gathering speed; he tried to hold back, his hands like vices around the brakes, but found himself forced to lean forward just to keep his balance. The earth was growing dryer and looser by the second and it was with a jolt that he realized that very near the surface was solid rock. The wind whipped tears from his eyes and prevented him from drawing breath. There was not much he could do now but concentrate on staying on the bike. His wheels began to bounce against the stones, and he found himself grating his teeth together as the pace seemed to quicken yet further. He was now hurtling down the mountainside out of control, his brakes unable to take the edge off the speed, and all he could do was concentrate on staying upright. It was around this time, as the wind began to howl around him like a trapped animal, that he felt his front wheel lose its grip and begin to slide. He instantly pulled his weight back, trying to prevent a full slide, only to feel the back wheel give in the same way. He concentrated on staying as sideways on as possible, knowing now that a crash-landing was inevitable, and tried to create some drag with his leg to slow his imminent fall.

With a blinding crack, his elbow met with a piece of rock jutting out from the earth and he was propelled forward and outward so that suddenly his bike was falling out from under him and the world began to whirl. It felt as if he was trapped in a giant washing machine, spinning round with incredible force, the ground coming up to slap him in the face at every turn. The firm knowledge that it would stop soon, that the ground would have to level out eventually, was of surprisingly little comfort. He closed his eyes, forced to submit to the inevitability of his roll, every crack sending shock waves of pain throughout his body and overriding any other sensation he could have possibly felt. It should have all been over in a few seconds, and in real time apparently it was, but his fall down the hillside seemed to last for ever. Something caught him hard above the ear and there seemed to be a moment of complete darkness before something else hit his knee, forcing him to acknowledge consciousness. And when the tumbling finally stopped, it took him by surprise and he thought he must still be rolling, although he could feel he was lying flat on the grass. He kept his eyes closed, teeth clenched, still expecting another hit, but none came. And it seemed he had been lying there for all eternity before he realized he was staring up at a brilliant blue sky.

It took him an age to get to his feet, and longer still to find his bike. He kept telling himself to hurry, hurry, hurry, but his body seemed to have its own agenda. As he finally recovered his bike and hobbled down to the edge of the road, he saw that he had torn a huge hole in the leg of his jeans, revealing a knee that was raw and bloody. His bare arms stung like crazy, there was something soft and sticky above his eye and his mouth tasted of blood . . . The relief he felt when he discovered his bike was still rideable was quickly replaced by breathtaking pain as he tried to push the pedals round on the smooth tarmac road.

It took him nearly an hour to ride into Windermere. A car pulled up at the side of the road and his heart almost stopped, but it was just a passer-by leaning out to ask if he was all right. Louis ignored him and pressed on, every push of the pedals sending a blinding pain through his knees. His mouth was dry and gritty, his body was plastered in sweat. And all he could think was *I've missed him, I've missed him, I've missed him*.

Outside the shiny modern Donex building in the centre of Windermere, Louis dropped his bike on the pavement, ignoring the horrified stares, and staggered into the lobby. He took the lift to the fourth floor, relieved to find it empty, and leaned dizzily against the smooth gold plaque of buttons, red blotches pulsating in front of his eyes. As the lift doors pinged open, he lurched into the corridor towards the receptionist's desk.

'I need to see Jonathan Franklin, it's an emergency . . .'

A horsy woman in a fitted violet suit stood up and said, 'Mr Franklin is in a meeting. Why don't you take a seat and I'll—'

'I need to see him now!' Louis shouted. 'Where is he?'

'I said he was in a meeting,' the woman repeated, glancing nervously towards a door on the left. 'If you could just take a seat, I'll see whether—'

Louis ran over to the door the woman had glanced at and threw it open. Seated round a long wooden table, a dozen or so men and women in suits were looking at a projection screen, next to which was standing—

'Dad!'

The suits all turned round. Dad's mouth dropped open. 'Louis! My God!' He moved quickly forwards. 'What's happened to you?' And then he froze.

'We've got to go,' Louis said, his voice shaking. '*Now.*'

Dad stared at him for a moment longer. Then,

suddenly, he snapped into action. Grabbing his briefcase, he muttered something about a family emergency and was propelling Louis back down the corridor. 'Where are the others?' he shouted as they ran down the stairs.

'They're waiting for us! We have to go and pick them up!'

They raced into the car park, Dad fumbling with the keys. His face was white and Louis could see that his hands were shaking. They slammed into the car and pulled out of the car park with a screeching of tyres.

'Don't get us stopped, Dad,' Louis warned him, bracing himself against the dashboard.

'Where are we going?'

'Down Whitely Road, to the fork that leads towards Grasmere.'

As they drove out of Windermere, Dad put his foot down and they raced back the way Louis had come, gobbling up in easy minutes the painful miles he had pedalled. Dad glanced over at him, sweat pearling on his forehead. 'What happened?' he asked. 'How?'

'Tell you later, Dad. Let's just get the others.' Louis' stomach was in knots again. They were over half an hour late.

'Are you all right, son? You're covered in blood! My God, what on earth happened?'

'I'm all right, Dad,' Louis said.

They came to a halt beside the church at the fork in the road and leaped out of the car. There was nothing but the twittering of birds and the distant hum of cars from the motorway. 'Oh, Christ, they're not here,' Louis choked.

The police car had been by to pick them up. Or else Millie had twisted her ankle jumping down from the tree. Either way, they were finished.

Dad looked at Louis in horror. Then a voice said, 'What the hell took you so long?'

They both swung round in surprise. Max was climbing out from behind a tall hedge, pulling Millie after him. Her face was streaked with tears. 'We thought you'd left us behind!'

'Thank God . . .' Dad breathed, grabbing the rucksacks from Max. 'Oh, thank God!'

They got into the car and Dad pulled away with another screech of tyres. After ten minutes of silence they were suddenly on the motorway.

'Where are we going?' Millie asked in a small, exhausted voice.

'I don't know,' Dad said quietly. 'I just don't know.'

Max turned round from the front seat and looked at Louis. 'Christ, what happened to you?'

'I had a bit of bumpy ride.' It hurt to talk.

'But you made it,' Max said with a smile. It was a smile that said, *I'm sorry*. It was a smile that said, *Thank you*.

Louis smiled back weakly, but felt only emptiness. He closed his eyes against the threat of tears. 'I made it,' he replied.

Epilogue

Louis lay beneath the duvet of the king-size double bed, staring up at the ceiling. The soft glow of the lamp cast a puddle of golden light on the pillow beside him. He could feel Dad's weight on the end of the bed and see his back, hunched forward, as he anxiously watched the ten o'clock news. Millie was curled up next to Louis on the bed, fast asleep, her hair still damp from the shower. Louis noticed that she didn't sleep sucking her two middle fingers any more. The slight chubbiness had gone from her cheeks, her face had elongated, and he suddenly realized how much she had changed since that snapshot on the missing-person's poster, how much she'd grown. Max lay sprawled diagonally across the other double bed, chin propped up on his hand, also gazing at the television. Louis didn't have the energy to move his head to look at the screen. But so far there had been nothing about an Anglo-French custody battle.

They had driven all day, only stopping for toilet breaks and food. Now they were in Scotland, in a place called Glasgow, in a hotel beside the airport. Tomorrow they would be taking the plane again. As usual, Dad wasn't saying where. Louis' skin still tingled from the hot bath. His badly scraped knee had been carefully cleaned and bandaged and Dad had managed to get some self-adhesive stitches for the deep gash across his eyebrow. He had swallowed some painkillers with a huge meal of pizza and Coke and now he felt achy and woozy and terribly tired. The newsreader's voice droned on. He turned his head on the pillow and looked at Millie's softly sleeping face. *I love you, Millie*, he thought.

The next morning Dad woke them up at the last minute. There was a tense few moments spent scrabbling round for clothes and checking under beds. But there wasn't really anything to pack. Dad promised them breakfast on the plane and they left their key at the empty reception desk and walked out of the sleeping hotel and into the cool dawn.

When they arrived at the near-empty check-in desk, the stewardess told them they would have to hurry. 'The flight to Amsterdam is about to board,' she said.

Amsterdam. Louis shot Max a wry smile. But there was no excitement any more.

This time there were no cartwheels in the waiting lounge. Millie sat huddled against Dad, her face pale and sleepy. Max, for once without his GameBoy, gazed out of the windows at the pink sunrise lighting up the sky. Dad was dishevelled and unshaven and looked like he hadn't slept. There were lines on his face that Louis didn't remember seeing before. His eyes were exhausted. He caught Louis looking at him and smiled. And suddenly Louis realized that love was a very powerful thing. It could make one man risk everything, even his freedom, just to be with his children.

Their plane was being called. Dad was urging them to gather their few remaining belongings. Louis handed Millie the second rucksack containing Dad's laptop as they followed the handful of other passengers down the mobile corridor towards the whirring mouth of the plane.

'But it's really heavy,' Millie complained.

'Just take it, Millie.'

Millie gave a dramatic roll of the eyes but took the rucksack from him without further fuss. The stewardess was getting ready to close the door of the plane as they arrived.

'Just in time,' she said. 'You're the last passengers.'

Max stepped through the opening and onto the plane. Dad took Millie's hand. Louis felt his heart lurch. He stepped back.

'Hurry, Louis,' Dad said, turning back in the doorway.

'I'm not coming,' Louis said.

'What?' Dad started to get off the plane again.

'Sir, we really have to close up now,' the stewardess said. 'Are you boarding this plane or not?'

'Yes,' said Dad. 'Yes! Louis, don't be silly, get on now!'

'No, Dad, I'm not coming,' Louis said again.

'What are you talking about?'

'What's going on?' Max had reappeared in the doorway. 'Is this our plane or not?'

'Louis says he doesn't want to come,' Dad said, a tremor in his voice.

Max gazed at Louis with a disbelieving smile on his face. 'What are you talking about? You want to stay in Glasgow?'

'I'm going back to live with Maman,' Louis said.

'Why?' Max asked in astonishment.

'I don't want to be doing this any more.'

'But we won't always be moving around, w-we're going to find a place, we're going to settle—' Dad was stammering.

'Sir, you're holding up the flight. I'm going to have to ask you to remove yourself from the doorway right now.'

'Fine, everyone off!' Dad snapped. 'We'll get another flight.'

'No way!' Louis moved quickly, blocking Dad's path. 'I nearly killed myself yesterday, and I didn't do it just for you to get caught!'

'But . . .'

'I'll see you when I'm sixteen, Dad.'

'Louis, please listen—'

'*Now*, sir!'

Dad's eyes were filling with tears. 'Are you serious? This is what you really want?'

Louis nodded.

'You've got Mum's number? You'll go straight back to the hotel and wait there till she comes to fetch you?'

'Yes, Dad, I promise.'

'And – and if you *ever* change your mind – I'll come and pick you up, Louis, anywhere! D'you understand?'

'I understand, Dad.'

'Sir—'

'Oh, Jesus!' Dad put his hand to his eyes, stumbled backwards and let the stewardess guide him into the aircraft.

'Look after him,' Louis said to Max.

Max stared at him. 'You're really not coming?'

'No.'

Millie suddenly shot out and grabbed Louis round the waist. He felt her sob into his T-shirt. Louis bent down and kissed the top of her head. 'Bye, Millie,' he whispered.

She wouldn't let go. He tried to loosen her arms from around his waist but she clung on tight. 'Millie, you've got to get on the plane. Dad needs you. I'll come and find you in a few years, I promise.'

Max reached down and pulled her firmly back. 'Millie, the plane's about to leave.' He looked up at Louis, his incredulous smile beginning to fade. 'I-I guess I'll see you in a year or so.'

Louis nodded.

'I'm really going to miss you!' Max said, his voice cracking.

'Me too.'

'Will you be OK?' Max asked.

'Yeah, I'll be fine.'

The stewardess began to close the door. 'I'll come and find you as soon as I'm sixteen!' Max said desperately, squeezing to the side.

'Yeah! See you, Max. See you, Millie.'

'Bye, Louis.' Max was forced back as the stewardess reached over and closed the door of the plane.

Louis stood in the airport lounge, in front of the glass wall, watching the plane taxi out onto the runway. He didn't move a muscle for the full ten minutes it took for the plane to get into position. The sound of the engines filled the air. He watched as the small aircraft accelerated down the runway, faster and faster, so that it was almost flying on the ground. The front wheels lifted off, and then it was airborne. Suddenly, the sky was empty, the air still resonating with sound. Louis stood frozen for several minutes longer, staring at the white morning sky. Slowly he raised his hands to his face and began to wipe away the tears.

Back in the main terminal, he dug some change out of his pocket and crossed to the row of empty phone booths that lined the wall. He picked up the brown plastic receiver and fed his change into the slot. Then he dialled a number – a number that he had thought about dialling so many times before.

There was a long pause before he was connected. Then a faint sound – the long ring from somewhere deep within the receiver. Then a click.

'*Allo?*'

A voice he knew. A voice weakened, more subdued than he remembered. But familiar all the same.

'Hello, Mum. It's Louis.'

Also by Tabitha Suzuma for older readers

A Note of Madness

by Tabitha Suzuma

Why is this happening to me?
he asked himself desperately.
What is wrong with me?

Life as a student should be
good for Flynn. He's one of the top pianists at the
Royal College of Music, he's been put forward for an
opportunity-of-a-lifetime concert, and he's got great
friends. But beneath the surface, he's falling apart.

On a good day he feels full of energy
and life, but on a bad day being alive is worse
than being dead. Sometimes he wants to compose
and practise all night, at other times he can't get
out of bed. With the pressure of the forthcoming
concert and the growing concern of his family
and friends, emotions come to a head.
Sometimes things can only get worse
before they get better.

978 0 099 48753 1

Also by Tabitha Suzuma for older readers

from where i Stand

tabithasuzuma

Raven is a deeply disturbed teenager. After witnessing the death of his mother and living in a children's home, he's now been placed in foster care. His new family, the Russells, do their best to earn his trust but it's going to take a long time.

Meanwhile, at school, bullies are making Raven's life a living hell. And then an unexpected saviour comes in the form of Lotte, a classmate bored by her 'ordinary' friends. Together, they set out to track down Raven's mum's killer, in order to expose him to the police. But their carefully crafted plan goes dangerously wrong and suddenly nothing is as it seems. Everything is falling apart, and ultimately there is only one, final, way out.

978 1 862 30212 9

Also by Tabitha Suzuma for older readers

A Voice in the Distance

by Tabitha Suzuma

Every thought hurts like hell. Everything you see is awful, twisted, pointless. And the worst – the worst of it is yourself.

Star pianist Flynn Laukonen has the world at his feet. He has moved in with his girlfriend Jennah and is already getting concert bookings for what promises to be a glittering career. Yet he knows he is skating on thin ice – only two small pills a day keep him from plunging back into the whirlpool of manic depression that once threatened to destroy him.

Suddenly Flynn finds himself in hospital, carnage left behind him. The medication isn't working any more and depression strikes again, this time with horrific consequences. It seems like he has to make a choice between the medication and his career. But in all this he has forgotten the one person he would give his life for, and Flynn suddenly finds himself facing the biggest sacrifice of all.

978 1 862 30355 3